11 Emerald Street

Hugh O'Donnell

WITHDRAWN FROM STOCK

JONATHAN CAPE
LONDON

Published by Jonathan Cape 2004

2 4 6 8 10 9 7 5 3 1

Copyright © Hugh O'Donnell 2004

Hugh O'Donnell has asserted his right under the Copyright, Designs
and Patents Act 1988 to be identified as the author of this work

This book is sold subject to the condition that it shall not,
by way of trade or otherwise, be lent, resold, hired out,
or otherwise circulated without the publisher's prior
consent in any form of binding or cover other than that
in which it is published and without a similar condition
including this condition being imposed on the
subsequent purchaser

First published in Great Britain in 2004 by
Jonathan Cape
Random House, 20 Vauxhall Bridge Road, London SW1V 2SA

Random House Australia (Pty) Limited
20 Alfred Street, Milsons Point, Sydney,
New South Wales 2061, Australia

Random House New Zealand Limited
18 Poland Road, Glenfield,
Auckland 10, New Zealand

Random House South Africa (Pty) Limited
Endulini, 5A Jubilee Road, Parktown 2193, South Africa

The Random House Group Limited Reg. No. 954009
www.randomhouse.co.uk

A CIP catalogue record for this book is
available from the British Library

ISBN 0-224-07182-3

Papers used by Random House are natural,
recyclable products made from wood grown in sustainable forests;
the manufacturing processes conform to the environmental
regulations of the country of origin

Typeset by Palimpsest Book Production Limited,
Polmont, Stirlingshire
Printed and bound in Great Britain by
Mackays of Chatham PLC

Leabharlann Chontae Laoise

Acc. No. 04/5240

Class No. F

Inv. No. 7434

To Ma and Da, with love

PART I

DA WAS RIGHT, you could smell fear. Brother Finch walked into the class on the stroke of nine – same as every Monday morning. The same fat face, the same bald shiny head.

'*Seasaigí.*' But this time there was no clattering of seats, just an awful silence as we all stood up to say our morning prayers. Everyone else must have been able to smell it too.

'*Sé do bheatha, a Mhuire*, Hail Mary, Holy Mary.' It was a lovely soft Irish prayer, but not the way we dragged it out that morning, dreading and waiting for the trouble to start. We all sat quietly, staring at the top of our desks, as if we'd never seen the old names carved into the wood or the stained inkwells before. We didn't have to wait long. You could hear his spidery writing on the blackboard.

'Here's the Fucker Finch!' and the crack as the chalk broke when he stabbed in that last exclamation mark.

'*Cé duirt é sin*? Who said that?' and the roar 'Last Friday on the train, the excursion – ye know.' His face was white as he smiled at us and went to sit on his big high chair. He squeezed both his hands together, and bent down to examine his shoes.

'O'Neill, where's the verb in that?' I nearly fainted with the mention of my name and I hoped the pain in my stomach wasn't diarrhoea.

'Present tense, the verb to be, abbreviated, is it sir?' He was tying a shoelace. He never looked up.

3

'Fox, where's the noun?'

'Finch, sir, capital noun, sir.' I hoped my voice hadn't sounded as terrified as his. His bald head nodded. There was no sound. Just the ticking of the clock. He lifted his head. He seemed to be staring past my right shoulder. Then an insane scream.

'Timmons, where's the adjective?' No answer. 'I can't hear you! I can't hear you, boy! Say it, boy. Say it loud. Like Friday! On the train. Remember it boy!' I could feel the breeze and smell his sweat as he leapt and ran past me across the top of the desks. He smashed Timmons on the face twice with his open hand before he had him on the ground. Timmons tried to block off the kicks. Timmons never cried. I felt such a terrible traitor as I thanked God it wasn't me.

Exhausted now, the Christian Brother walked back up the class. He never looked back. He just walked out and didn't slam the door.

It always seemed like a magical address, '11 Emerald Street'. I loved writing it carefully on the top left-hand side of the cream Belvedere Bond writing paper that my ma insisted we use for sending letters. I used to love writing letters with that magical address. I even got a penpal from the *Our Boys* magazine that we had to buy in school. 'Martin Flaherty, Nobber, County Meath'. Just that. No street name. I should have guessed by the lousy address that he'd get me into trouble. But that was later and I had two whole months of summer stretching ahead without poxy Brother Finch and all the lovely trips to Bray and Howth and Dollymount, and even Fairview Park when my da's holiday money would be gone.

Even our street sign was magic. Deep green with 'Emerald Street' in white letters – a bit rusty, but perfectly placed high up on the side wall of the corner house for practising your hurling with a worn tennis ball.

4

I could always hit it spot on except on those summer Friday evenings, when most of the kids would be in for their tea, and I'd be waiting for my da to swing around the far corner in his blue mechanic's overalls, fighting the drink to stay on his bike.

You can't do two jobs at once, and I'd often whack the ball off Granny Wilson's window by accident when I'd see him out of the corner of my eye, and I'd break the world record for soloing a tennis ball on a hurley and grab the bike before they both fell.

I never wanted the Barretts to see him drunk. They were my big enemies, especially Pat the bully with the airgun, same age but much bigger than me. One day I was trying to hypnotise him into giving me a go with the gun. My grand uncle Mick gave me the hypnotist book, but maybe because I didn't do the swinging watch thing, or hadn't painted on the beard like the man in the book, Barrett went mad.

'Who are you fuckin' starin' at?' and he shot me in the knee. Then he put the gun to my neck. 'Swear you'll follow Liverpool.' Luckily my ma came out then 'cos I'd already promised my older brother Tommy that I'd be a true blue Evertonian if he'd write an anonymous letter to Brother Finch threatening to give him a dig. My ma was going to sue the Barretts but Tommy gave him a good hiding and there was a temporary ceasefire.

Those summer Saturdays were even worse 'cos my da got a half day then and all my gang would be out playin' twenty-a-side street soccer. No matter how many times I'd say, 'Next goal the winner,' I could never get them to finish before Da would swing onto the street in the black Citroën car he'd be out test-driving as a nixer for a weekend customer. Most of the neighbours knew it was a dangerous time to stand on the footpath but guessed the kids'd be safe on the road. Sure enough, on the stroke of three, the afternoon madness would start. The screech of brakes as the black car swung sharp, bounced hard on the kerb and raced down the path. Even Granny Wilson (who must have been eighty) would leap like a gazelle inside her front door. Then all the football would stop.

'Giz a lift, Mr O'Neill, ah g'wan, give us a spin.' I'd be like a general picking his bravest as we'd squeeze maybe fifteen of us into the Citroën for the test run. I never invited the Downeys. They were the only ones on the street with their own car, a clapped out Ford that we called the Golden Carriage 'cos they'd never give you a ride. I was so popular then, and I'd get great comic swaps from the chosen many for the great adventure. I'd always ask Pat Barrett if he wanted to come. I don't know why. Maybe because I guessed correctly that my older brother Tommy wouldn't always be around. But he'd always have the same sneer and the same answer, as I sat in the front seat with my three best pals.

'Your da is bottled' and I'd tell him to fuck off. Luckily the engine would be racing and my da would never hear him.

'Robbie, what's wrong with young Barrett?'

'He's got the measles, Da, his ma won't let him go.' (I'd always give the same excuse.)

'Poor kid.' Nought to sixty in seven seconds, a final bounce off the kerb, the kids begin to scream. 'He should go to the doctor,' my da would say. 'It's lasting an awful long time!'

That summer went too fast. Just my week to that strange address – Nobber, County Meath – my da's holidays, then back to the Fucker Finch. My penpal looked older than I'd imagined and was trying to grow a moustache. I hated him right away. He told me I could call him Marty and asked me if I'd ever kissed a girl. There was definitely a smell of country off him, but at least I had my own room.

6

By the third day I was sick of all the gristly meat and pitch dark nights – not even one car went by – and the next day he took me into the field to show me something. Two horses were at it. I'd never seen this before. He was grinning and explaining stuff. When I looked around he had his thing out and said he wanted to do it to me. His was much bigger than mine and I got such a fright I kicked him hard with my new confirmation shoes and made it bleed and you should have seen it shrink.

My ma'd hardly ever let me wear my confirmation shoes, especially playing football on the street, but she'd said to take them with me to the country that week and not let myself down, and thank God for that. I was sent home that night on the bus with a note for my ma. All the way back to Dublin, looking out through the bus window at the rain, I couldn't wait to see the city lights, and I knew I'd never give that note to my ma. So I tore it into tiny pieces and walking home from the bus station I put the bits in different rubbish bins and kept looking around to make sure I wasn't being followed. I just told my ma that my penpal Martin had got the measles, and they thought it was better to be safe than sorry. My da said there was an awful lot of that going around.

I stayed awake very late that night listening to the trucks and the cars going down to the docks, and the people laughing on their way out of Noctor's pub, and even though my younger brother Shea had wet the bed, I was very glad to be home.

There was no clean sheets dry in our house because it had been raining all that week when I was away, so I just put newspapers under me. Shea was fast asleep and wouldn't even notice and anyway he always blamed me. There was still a smell of country off my hands even though I'd washed them three times with the Sunlight

7

soap that only Ma and my sisters were allowed to use. It was too early to hear all the trucks and horses and carts and the tooting horns from the factories that I loved waking up to so I tried to see if I could still remember all the streets in our parish. Talbot Street, near where Da worked, was great, specially near Christmas with all the toys in the shops and the Christmas lights that the men would spend weeks putting up but would take them down too early, even before you had a chance to walk up there on your way to the pantomime in the Gaiety that Uncle Paul always paid for in January 'cos it was cheaper. And it was so cold then – even the man with the hump who sold shoelaces on the Boundary Wall probably went home to his ma, 'cos he was never there at Christmas. Nor was Apple Annie who'd hide under the arches with her cider bottle and curse at you if you even looked at her. It was very dangerous to cycle down there on Da's bike, especially in the rain on the cobbles. I didn't fall even once although Da often came home from his work with bumps and bruises giving out hell about the flipping cobbles, though Ma didn't really believe him and blamed it on the Guinness he used to drink nearly always on a Friday night and that wasn't even on the Boundary Wall, that was in Noctor's in Sheriff Street near the flats, where you'd take your life in your hands delivering the Catholic papers for the Legion of Mary.

There was always a smell of bacon and cabbage in some of the flats that would make you sick, and the men would come out in their sweaty vests to take in the paper without paying, saying the missus wasn't in. Except skinny Mrs Grigson in 7B who had fourteen kids but she would always pay you on time. Then you had to race past Clicky Kelly and his gang. He had a hatchet and he'd threaten to scalp you if he caught you but he never did. Sometimes the money would go missing, even when I hid it in the

8

brown press in the parlour, because Da must have had a key but I never worried about that 'cos I knew Ma'd always fix it up. Anyway the drink is supposed to be a disease and not their fault and Da wasn't to blame. And maybe it wasn't him because my younger brother Shea always seemed to have more money than me, or even my older brother Tommy because he always had money to take his girlfriends out to posh teas in the Savoy Grill.

But the rain still poured down outside on Emerald Street that night, and the newspaper on my side of the bed was getting a bit damp. I was beginning to forget about the country now, and could remember everything about my street. I knew every crack on the pavement and how many hops it took to get to Darcy's shop on the corner, but you had to be very careful doing that in case the money for the messages would fall out of your pocket and roll down the shore outside Merrigan's house. And our house, number eleven, right in the middle with the green door and the black goat's head for a doorknocker with the letter box that had to be shined up with Brasso every Saturday morning before you could go out to play.

Everyone said our doorknocker was like the devil's head and very unlucky. Sometimes it was, specially when the neighbours would come hammering on it to give out hell about me. Mrs Kelly from Oriel Street because I'd split her son's head with a big stick, which I did, and Mrs Downey for dragging her daughter down the back lane and pulling down her knickers, which I definitely didn't do, that was my younger brother Shea. But I never squealed on him and got a terrible thumping from Ma because she hated that stuff. I never got the credit from Shea that I deserved, and Shea never even told me what it looked like, and maybe it was remembering about that or all that stuff about the horses in the country that made me do it, 'cos when I got up to find a dry newspaper I saw my sister fast asleep across the room and I decided to have a peep for myself. But she turned in her sleep and I was shaking so much now, and even though I never found out, it was a grievous matter with clear knowledge and full consent and it was a terrible mortal sin.

I hardly slept at all that night and it wasn't the wet bed. I was serving seven mass the next morning and though Father Williams was deaf and half blind, he must have been fifty years in the business and they were all trained to spot a black soul from fifty yards, even the new ones with shiny faces. And in confession, they always knew when you were holding back. 'Have you any more sins to confess, my son?' But this was so bad I could never tell anyone, so I just tried to forget it. The next morning when Father Williams was skipping through the Latin real fast and racing towards the communion, I remembered I couldn't receive and then he'd tell Ma 'cos they were great friends and she'd want to know why. I even forgot to ring the bells for the Sanctus, but at least he was deaf and wouldn't notice. But he did and turned and muttered something about the water and wine that I'd forgotten about as well. I was in such a rush that I nearly knocked the little cruets over. Then I saw my chance. There was only one old man waiting at the altar rails and it wasn't Uncle Mick so I'd probably get away with it.

'No one for communion, Father.' The lie was still a sin but only a venial one. Going to communion with a mortal sin on your soul was a sacrilege that only the Archbishop could forgive and he mightn't even do that and excommunicate you for life or until you were sixty-five.

'*Ita missa est*,' said the priest and when I said, '*Deo Gratias*!' I really really meant it.

That was the day I decided to become a Prod. They could read the Bible themselves and make up their own minds what was a sin, and even though Brother Finch used laugh at their foolishness and say they'd all die in torment, I decided to give it a go. Sure, wasn't Hattie Hobson a Prod, and she was really popular with all the older lads on our street. Even Bantam, the biggest boy in our class, used to take her on picnics, and her ma and da were always laughing. They always seemed to be loaded. I could always switch back at the last minute, no harm done, and say a Perfect Act of Contrition. My only problem now was Father Williams. He was the only priest who knew my ma real well, and he'd tell her for certain that I wasn't fulfilling my religious duties, and though I swear I never prayed for it, didn't he drop dead that week of a massive heart attack, and my problems were gone. The only thing was I couldn't tell anyone, only my best pal Kevin and he told his ma and his ma told my ma and there was murder. So I just denied the whole shagging thing.

My da told me that when I was older I could make up my mind for myself but in the meantime it'd be no harm to read the Bible, 'cos there was a lot in it, and he bought me one for my birthday even though I really wanted a mouth organ. But I couldn't let him down so I read it from cover to cover – Matthew and Mark were OK but I liked Luke the best. I tried John but there was a lot of stuff in there about sins of the flesh so I gave it a miss. Then one day Hattie Hobson told me the Prods only read King James. I couldn't believe it, I'd wasted ages on the wrong stuff. She told me she'd lend me a James one if I gave her some of my older sister's *School Friend* comics. I did and there was a huge row but it was worth it 'cos I was getting on brilliant with Hattie Hobson now and even Bantam and Barrett were jealous, and I think she even liked me.

One day I told my older brother Tommy about it and that was a big mistake. Next thing I knew he became a

Prod too and started asking her out. They went everywhere together and he gave me that wink which meant I couldn't tell Ma. She even went to see him playing football for O'Connell Boys. OK, he was good, but that was the end of my new girlfriend. I was so annoyed and disappointed about the whole thing that I decided to give up being a Prod.

Bantam told me about this deaf priest so I got the bus out to the church in Finglas one Saturday morning. There were millions of people waiting outside his confession box, mainly men, but they all seemed to go in and out really quick. When my turn came I wasn't even nervous and I muttered the whole lot out in one breath. One Hail Mary for penance? The man was a saint! I felt so relieved and happy when I came out until I saw the mother of one of my best friends, Jimmy Jackson, waiting anxiously to go in. I couldn't even guess what she was doing there; maybe she followed me on the bus. Anyway Jimmy Jackson was not allowed play with me again for ages.

But that didn't bother me too much 'cos he always smelt sweaty. There was always a lot of gossip about his family because they kept themselves to themselves. One day I heard two of our neighbours talking about them when they thought I wasn't listening. I was sitting on the kerb making a raft out of lollipop sticks. One of them was saying wasn't it strange they didn't call Jimmy, their only son, Oliver, after the da, and that there was no resemblance between father and son. And wasn't it a bit odd the way Mrs Jackson went to communion every day but never went to confession. I knew the answer to that. I'd seen her with the deaf priest in Finglas but I wasn't going to tell them that.

My next girlfriend was Marian Casey, but she wouldn't admit it. She had curly black hair and green eyes and I never saw anyone so beautiful. Now that I was back in the fold, I could serve mass again, and I always put my name down for the ten o'clock on Sunday morning 'cos that's when she'd always go. And when she'd be kneeling for communion I'd always rub the silver patten gently under her chin, to let her know how I felt. I admired the way she always kept her eyes closed in prayer, pretending nothing had happened. It was her way of letting me know she was mad about me. David, her brother, never knew why I was so friendly with him and always called to his house to swap marbles and give him a great deal. The odd time she'd answer the door, she'd keep the pretence going by leaving me outside in the rain for hours and forgetting to tell him who was there. She mustn't have wanted her ma to know anything about the relationship. I kept it quiet at home too and certainly never mentioned it to my older brother Tommy.

Shea and Tommy had curly hair and I began to realise that girls must love that because my new girlfriend Marian Casey never left Shea waiting outside their door. There was only one thing to do so one night when my older sister was asleep I borrowed her hair curlers. I waited until everyone was asleep and had a go in front of the mirror in the back kitchen. There usen't be shampoo then, but when I mixed up the Ajax powder into a paste it seemed to work. My hair curled up really fast. But when it started to burn and sting I got afraid and knew I'd made a mistake. I tried to wash it off, but there was only a trickle from the cold tap. The jacks outside was better but I had to put my head right down into the bowl and couldn't really reach the ceiling flush chain. My ma hadn't got much sleep that night with all the coughing from her asthma, but when I woke her to help me she never said a word – just boiled up the kettle and worked out the mess and gave me money for a haircut in Mickey Wellington's, and never even gave out to me when I came back with a crewcut.

Tommy was the brains of the family and I wasn't too bad but Shea couldn't be bothered about that stuff. He had red hair and a temper to match. He used to suck his thumb much longer than the rest of us and me and Tommy used to call him 'sucky thumb' if we wanted to annoy him and get him to give us a chase, although you'd never say it in front of his pals and let him down. He had twinkling blue eyes and all the girls used to love him and that'd annoy me so much. One day when everyone was out somewhere, I was practising the piano in the parlour with one finger and I heard him laughing outside on the street. He was practising kissing with Sheila Merrigan and Lily Downey, the girl whose knickers he'd pulled down and wouldn't tell me what he saw. When he came in for his dinner I'd eaten most of it, and he nearly went mad. He was using new curse words that he must have learnt from our cousin Dermot. I couldn't resist it so I swore back at him with stuff I'd learnt from our other cousin Damian. I called him a hoor's melt. That didn't seem to bother him. Then I made a big mistake. I called him sucky thumb and told him he was a big sissy to be playing with girls.

I should have known to go into hiding at once the way his face went red. He ran out of the kitchen and grabbed a huge hammer from Uncle Mick's toolbox in the back kitchen and I could hear the 'fuck!'s of him as he came looking for me. Luckily the kitchen table was huge and I kept throwing chairs in his way as he chased me around it. There was no stopping him now and he missed my head with the hammer by just a few inches about four times, and he kept getting closer. I don't know how but I jumped over the table and out the kitchen

14

door in a flash and locked myself in the parlour. The way he was belting on the lock with the hammer, I knew it wouldn't hold and that he'd never give in, so I opened the parlour window and climbed out over the rose thorns and fell onto the street. I was bleeding from all the cuts and my foot got twisted on the railing spikes, but at least I'd escaped and hopped all the way down around the corner and sat on the Hogans' steps. Tom Hogan was there already playing his guitar in the sun. When I told him what had happened he said his younger brother Gordon was the same and the best way out was to bribe or black-mail them. I didn't have any money so when I finally went home I told Shea I'd tell Ma about Lily Downey's knickers and that seemed to calm him down. But I never called him sucky thumb again, and he stopped doing that soon after, when Da put mustard on his thumb when he was asleep.

One day he became a big hero in our parish for at least a month. He'd been annoying me over something and I gave him the hardest Legion of Mary job all on his own, to deliver the Sunday Catholic papers into Bridget's Garden flats. He'd never done it before and didn't know as much as I did about Clicky Kelly and his gang. Anyway, he was only starting off in B block and didn't a three-year-old kid fall off the second balcony just as Shea was walking past and he dropped the papers in the muck and caught her safely. His picture was all over the newspapers that week and the girls were even madder after him than ever.

All the women on the street said my older sister Elaine was like a film star she was so beautiful, and she had no problem getting herself boyfriends. One day three of them came up to me in Fairview Park and told me to tell her they'd love to play with her golliwog. I ran straight home with the exciting news. I knew she'd be delighted because I think she fancied one of them, and anyway I didn't know she had a golliwog and must have kept it hidden in her bedroom. She was helping Ma with the washing-up when I told her the great news. It was the hardest slap on the face I ever got and I was sent crying to my bedroom. I could hear the terrible row below, then Elaine thumped up the stairs and banged on my door calling me a telltale bastard and wouldn't talk to me for a week. I felt really bad because she'd never let you down no matter what trouble you'd be in and always stick up for you and I was delighted for her later on when she got the new boyfriend Joe Connolly that Ma liked, I think 'cos he drove a truck and his ma and da were from the country. He even had a car and would take Ma up to Glasnevin to visit the graves, and he was a great footballer and nearly played for Dublin once.

I'd do anything for my younger sister Mary Joe. She had a teddy bear called Bruno. She'd bring him every-where with her and it was always getting worn out. I'd always go up to the doll's hospital with her and wait when he was in getting fixed. She wouldn't leave him in overnight so we'd have to hang around for hours. While we were waiting we'd go into Walton's, the music shop, and they'd let you play on the big pianos, and even the drums, until it was time to collect Bruno. Elaine must have left her golliwog in to be fixed in the doll's hospital and forgot to collect him because I never saw him in our house even though one day when everyone was out I searched all over her room.

Anyway I had to keep writing to that bollix in Nobber because Ma said it would be very bad manners not to after they'd been so good to me. He even got a pal of his to write to Shea, but I knew if Shea was ever invited down there I'd have to warn him off. Then his ma and my ma started writing to each other nearly every week. It was like the whole family was going mad writing and all the Belvedere Bond paper was being used up really fast. It was autumn and we were back at school. We were miles away from Christmas and we'd got poxy Finch again for another year, but something great happened.

One day when I came home from school, Ma was so excited she'd forgot to keep me any stew. The Nobber woman had wrote to her saying that they had a lovely black and white collie puppy that they wanted me to have. She must have been reading all my letters to him with the secret code about horses and thought I needed a pet. I read her spidery writing. If we went down straight away we could have it for free. Da borrowed a big Citroën from his garage that Saturday. I was a bit nervous about the whole idea, but at least Ma and Da were with me and Mary Joe and Shea. I really wanted that puppy and I knew I'd call him Bobby 'cos that was like my name. Tommy and Elaine were delighted to have the house to themselves. They were up early that morning helping with the breakfast. I had to make sure that Da wouldn't sneak off to an early house for Guinness so I locked him in the parlour till everything was ready and he nearly went mad. Uncle Mick wanted to know what all the thumping and hammering was all about. I had to fib so I told him Shea was making a new wooden house for our new dog which was a terrible big lie because Shea couldn't nail two planks together.

Everything was nearly ready now. Ma had made loads of crisp and banana and tomato sandwiches. Everything seemed very quiet and peaceful in the parlour when I went to let Da out. But the window was open and no sign of Da. Me and Shea ran up to Noctor's. We hated going in there because it was Da's pub and you'd be letting him down. Da was sitting on his bar stool with his Guinness and a big red mark on his forehead. He never said a word, just threw back the Guinness with one big swallow. The barman shouted after him, 'Enjoy the country, Jim,' and he limped after us out the door. He must have had the same trouble as me climbing out the parlour window. Ma was so busy getting ready she never noticed the injuries, or maybe she didn't want to start a row. On the way down the country, Da's kidneys were at him so we had to stop a few times before we even reached the Red Cow pub just past Inchicore. But we weren't late because Da was a really fast driver and we only had to stop one more time to let Ma out to get sick and sit in the back.

It was funny being down there again with all my family. It still had the country smell but they were all very nice to us. They even brought Shea's new penfriend over to meet him. He looked really young and certainly wouldn't be causing Shea any problems with his thing. And Bobby was the most beautiful dog I ever saw.

Da wasn't used to country butter and he cut a huge slab of it off and gave it to Bobby. On the way home after Bobby got sick over everyone Ma wanted to know what the hell Da had been up to and Da said he thought it was a big lump of cheese. We had to put Bobby in the boot because he kept getting sick. Da was very good and didn't stop even once on the way back. I had to give Bobby a bath in the tub in the back kitchen and it was freezing down there. But Uncle Mick lit a big fire and wrapped him in an old towel to stop him shivering. Ma said he could sleep there all night. I wanted to take him for a walk but Da said it wouldn't be fair – just let him settle and get used to us – so I borrowed a thick black marker from Elaine and wrote 'Bobby' in big letters on both sides of my hurley. Later that night when

Ma was sweeping up the kitchen floor Bobby started snarling like mad and Tommy said he must have got a good few hidings from a brush and what sort of people were we all writing to.

I couldn't tell him then but I did later in the bedroom, and he swore he wouldn't tell Ma, but something must have happened because Ma never wrote to the spidery woman from Nobber again, and neither did me or Shea.

The first time out on the lead was terrible. Bobby pulled and dragged so hard he kept choking himself and everyone was looking at us so I had to carry him all the way to Fairview Park. I was really tired so the minute we got inside the gate I let him off and he was gone like a bullet across a men's proper football match with everyone in jerseys and a referee. He tried to bite the referee's ankles and then ran up over the hill towards the railway track. The referee made a kick at me as I ran after him as fast as I could. Then he got into a mad fight with a man with a huge greyhound on a lead. I finally managed to grab him up and the man said if I didn't fuck off out of the park the pair of us, his greyhound would have my fucking dog for breakfast. As I carried him home Bobby seemed happy enough, except every time we passed anyone in black he'd snarl and show his teeth. Then I remembered that the referee and the greyhound man who told us where to go were all dressed in black. And it suddenly dawned on me – the spidery woman from Nobber was a widow and always wore black. Tommy was right, she must have always been bashing him with a brush and maybe even kicking him. And sure enough, when I got home Uncle Willy had called in on his way home from a funeral and Bobby nearly bit the arse off him, and poor oul Uncle Willy hadn't done a thing wrong.

After that we had to keep Bobby out in the backyard when any visitors were coming, in case they wore the wrong colour, and Uncle Mick had to buy a new light-grey Sunday suit and kept muttering it made him look like mutton dressed as lamb, but he wore it to mass every Sunday anyway, and Granny Wilson even stopped him once and told him he was still a very handsome man, and wasn't it a pity the rest of the men on the street wouldn't folly his example and not let themselves go. Uncle Mick said he wasn't happy about that at all and that Granny Wilson must be eighty-three if she's a day and it'd match her better to be going to a second mass instead of ogling the men, but I think he was a bit pleased.

But the priests with their jet-black suits had no chance and stopped calling around for their Christmas and Easter dues and Da said sure there was no harm in that and gave Bobby one of his chops. Mr Merrigan who lived five doors away next to Hattie Hobson had a huge dog kennel that was empty. Their big Alsatian had died a year ago and everyone suspected that Mrs Hobson had poisoned him for howling. Anyway he gave it to us for free. Bobby loved it in the backyard. It was all concrete with a few big cracks and Ma had a little wooden box on stilts out there with a metal grille and tiny holes so when she put the Sunday meat out there in the summer it would last until nearly Tuesday except when Tommy would cut big slices off for himself and I'd give the fat bits to Bobby. The only toilet in the whole house was out there too and it didn't have any electricity. So when any visiting men wearing black went out there I'd have to go out and hold Bobby back.

We put Bobby's house in the farthest away corner near the coal shed and he'd let our two cats Paddy and Joey sleep in there with him even though they were black. Bobby could scent things from miles away specially if he was lying in the hall waiting for me to come home. He had a special whine the minute Clicky Kelly stepped into our street so you'd know it wasn't safe to go out. He had a different one for Da. It was two different yelps and you knew if you ran straight out the hall door into Emerald Street that Da had just turned the corner on his way home. The only bad thing was even when he was in the backyard and we were playing in the street, if I put a foot into Sheriff Street he'd start howling and Ma'd know I'd disobeyed orders – we were never allowed go up there before you were eleven and you'd be in big trouble if you did. And it wasn't fair because Shea got away with it loads of times.

There was a playground up there with swings and slides and a nice man called Mr Gallagher who wouldn't let anyone thump you. And for years before I got Bobby, I'd play in there all day and never get caught out. Except the day I was standing waiting to get on the swings some-body pushed me from behind and next thing a boy on the swings with callipers on him smashed my head and his iron boot got caught in my green jumper that Ma had just knitted, and dragged me along the ground. There was blood everywhere and Mr Gallagher carried me home with loads of kids following. There was so much blood Ma was afraid to thump me and we both walked up to the chemist. But the chemist man said he could do nothing for me and I needed stitches so we walked up to Temple Street Hospital. Ma was walking very fast and saying nothing. I was looking behind me at a boy who passed by with toy handcuffs and a policeman's badge and gun and when Ma called me to hurry up I turned straight away into a green lamp-post and nearly lost an eye. We had to get a taxi then and the man in the taxi said I must be terrible accident prone and gave Ma his hankie to stop the gushing. The nurse in the hospital was really nice and washed away the blood very gently before she gave me the injections. Then she took off her watch and put it on my arm while she was taking my pulse. I thought it was a present for being very brave and didn't want to give it back. When we got home that night my head was covered in bandages and Da got a terrible fright. Anyway I think that was the main reason we weren't allowed go into Sheriff Street any more. But we didn't have Bobby then so I could never figure out how he knew it was so dangerous.

Uncle Mick told me he got the hypnotist book off a cattle drover, who learned how to put the cows asleep on the ship when it got very stormy, and they'd be very upset. He'd just stare into their eyes and tap them on the forehead and down they'd go. I'd read it a good few times and practised on Bobby and our cats but they'd never stay still long enough. The Downeys' black mongrel was too old and always sleeping in the sun anyway so he was no use. Uncle Mick was great – he said he'd let me practise on him. I'd been trying out my deep voice on Shea but he kept grinning and sticking out his tongue. But Uncle Mick sat quietly in his chair and I had my favourite conker tied on a string for the swinging part. It worked really quick. He was fast asleep in seconds, even snoring, so I knew he wasn't messing. His mouth was open and there was a little bit of tobacco juice running down his jaw and he was twitching a bit. 'Uncle Mick, when you wake up you're going to give me sixpence for the pictures.' I said it slowly, three times, just like it said in the book. Then I tapped him gently on the forehead. 'Wake up!' 'What? Where am I? What happened! Oh it's you son. Here – here's a tanner for the pictures.' I couldn't believe how well it worked – God, I'd easy get the price of my own bike off him that I was saving up to buy at the police auction – I'd just have to get time with him alone. Then Shea came in and immediately Uncle Mick gave him a tanner for the pictures too. That wasn't supposed to happen so I spent the whole night reading the book again to see what had gone wrong. But at least I knew I could be a hypnotist if I wanted to. That night Uncle Mick gave all my brothers and sisters a tanner and I knew he'd be broke really soon so I decided never to do that to him again.

To make it up to Uncle Mick I promised I'd go to Glasnevin with him to visit his wife's grave. He was really old but could still walk fast enough. It had a lovely head-stone on it with a tiny hedge all the way round and her name was Ellen. We didn't have to say too many prayers and when we were walking back he told me all about her and how they had taken Ma and her sisters in when their ma and da died. He never said much about my da but he liked Ma a lot. I wanted to find one of the vaults where you could look in the railings and see a real coffin. We were standing outside one where there were loads of people praying and I'm sure I heard Uncle Mick muttering, 'I'm as much a saint as anyone — Matt Talbot me arse!'

Ma had to put up with an awful lot from me, especially when I decided to become a faith healer. It was an ad on the back page of the *Irish Press*:

Finbar Nolan — Faith Healer.
Seventh son of a seventh son.
Carlton Hall, Fairview. 8 p.m. Tuesday 5th March.
Admission 5 shillings.

I couldn't believe it. I really couldn't. I was good at sums and worked out that if only a hundred people turned up, that was twenty-five pounds! Three times my da's wages in just one night. And his picture — he looked just like me although I was only the second son of a second son. I knew immediately this was for me. I'd already practised loads of times on my da. He'd have a massive headache on Sunday mornings, and when he'd go back to sleep after his dinner (the Hobsons called it lunch), I'd put my hand on his head and when he got up it would always be gone. It never failed. And another time when we were playing rugby in Fairview Park and Freddy Wentworth crashed into me, I collapsed onto the grass just lying there having a massive heart attack. But I just breathed in deeply and cured myself and got up slowly and only got sick once and kept on playing. But now, reading the ad, I got so excited and knew I was going to leave school immediately, and buy my ma a new house – maybe even with a garden – where my da could retire and train racing pigeons and I'd look after them forever and we'd all have a bedroom each and I'd even buy my older sister Elaine a record player and three Buddy Holly records. And not only fix headaches. I'd teach cripples to walk, cure the blind, even raise the dead! That last one was when my ma got really worried and said I was blasphemous or mad and that something terrible would happen to me.

I hated birds. I couldn't bear it when they'd charge at you and flutter if you went too near their nests on the canal. Maybe when I was a baby in my pram one of them swooped down and stole an ice cream I was sucking or a lollipop. Some of the lads from the flats used to keep pigeons. They'd sit at the corner of our street and leave twine out with a loop at the end. Then they'd put bits of corn all over it and around it. It was easy to rob corn from Dolan's warehouse but they didn't need much of it anyway. When the pigeons would step inside the loop they'd pull it hard and catch it by the legs and the pigeon would fly up in the air in a big circle trying to escape and swing wild near their heads until they hauled it in. I never went near them when they were doing that. If they found out you were afraid of birds they'd torture you for the rest of your life and blackmail your sling or your money off you or whatever else you had in your pocket.

That was the one thing I hated about Christmas. Our cousins from Wexford would send you up a big parcel with a big home-made Madeira cake and a live goose in a separate box with holes for air. Me and Shea had to carry it down to the butcher's we didn't really like, because he always tried to cheat Ma before we got the new one, and he'd kill it and clean it and we'd have to leave it hanging upside down from the clothes line in the back kitchen. It was a terrifying sight and there was no way I'd go down there on my own at night-time to wash my teeth or fill up the kettle. Da said it was the living you'd want to be afraid of, not the dead, and he'd go down there with you when it was your turn to make the tea. He'd swing the goose when you weren't looking and start cackling like one and frighten the living daylights out of you.

But that Christmas week when the postman knocked with the parcel I was in the house on my own, polishing up the lino in the hall for Ma. I loved that job. You just spread the Cardinal Clear polish all over first, then you got a pair of Da's woolly socks that had been darned so much from all the singes because Ma had forgotten to take them out in time from the big black oven beside the fireplace. One night Ma had forgotten and left all our underpants in all night. They were burnt to a cinder and we had to go around all Sunday without any. Ma was terrified we'd have an accident and be knocked down by a car and have to go to hospital so we were hardly let out at all that day. Da's socks were brilliant for sliding. If you ran back a bit you could slide the whole way up to the hall door.

Then the postman knocked and I couldn't believe it was the shagging parcel from the country. There was nothing I could do. I had to sign for it and take it in. The goose was going wild inside the box and I held it as far away from me as I could. I didn't even see the cat. I tried real hard to stay on my feet but I'd done too good a job on the floor. The box crashed hard against the banister and the feckin' goose was out. It was huge with massive white wings and was scooting all over the shiny floor. I was screaming with fright. Then it started eating lumps out of the Madeira cake. At least it was distracted. I crept past it and out the hall door like a shot. I ran down the street and knocked hard on Tom Daly's door – the boy with the bare feet.

'Please dear God let him be in please – oh Jaysus c'mon, answer the door.' I walked back slowly but I'd locked myself out so I had to run down the back lane, climb into Billy Cartwright's yard and over our back wall. At least Bobby was there and he was from the country so he should know how to kill a goose. I opened the back door into the house and peeped in. Everything seemed quiet enough but I couldn't see anything in the hall. I crept in really slowly. I had my hurley with me this time.

It must have been waiting for me and came straight for my face in a white blur. I took a swing at it and missed, but at least it ran out into the yard. Then Bobby got to work and it was like World War Two. Then I got a great idea – I opened the door of the coal shed wide. I grabbed a big lump of butter from the safe where it was always kept and between me and Bobby and the hurley and the butter, we got the poxy thing into the coal shed and slammed the door. I rushed back all over the house picking up the feathers and the crumbs of cake and did my best to tidy up the place but I couldn't take my mind off the monster out there in the coal shed.

Thank God Da came home first. I was talking so fast he couldn't hear a word I said. Finally he got the message. I wanted him to go out there and kill the bastard and we'd hang it up on the line in the back kitchen and Ma would be none the wiser. He seemed a bit reluctant but I begged him so much he said he'd have a go. There's no light in our coal shed. It's very big and you have to climb in. Da opened the door very cautiously. He had a big rope in his hand, I don't know why. Maybe he was going to hang him then and there. He climbed in carefully and said, 'Keep the hurley handy – just in case.' The minute he was inside there was a huge screech from the goose. I slammed the door shut with fright. You never heard anything like the roars of Da. I thought he was shouting at the goose. Then I realised it was me.

'Open the fucking door!' He'd never ever cursed at me before. I swung it open fast and he fell out. 'Shut it – shut it quick for God's sake! It's a fucking gander,' and I did. Da was covered in coal dust and there was white feathers in his hair. They mustn't have had ganders on his farm when he was young. Maybe only chickens. Da went to tidy himself up, and came back out with a different plan. But Uncle Mick saved the day. He'd been working all night and was just out of bed and when we told him the problem he started laughing at Da and I think Da was a bit annoyed. Uncle Mick went off and got a coal sack and told me and Da to help him into the shed. It took only a few minutes and you couldn't hear a sound. Then out came Uncle Mick delighted with himself holding up the dead prize. They washed all the coal off it in the back kitchen, and stuffed it into a big cardboard box. I got Kevin O'Farrell to help me carry it down to the butcher's. They mustn't have said a thing to Ma because she kept saying she was more than surprised that our cousins from Wexford hadn't bothered to send up the cake.

I think Uncle Mick hated Christmas. Maybe it reminded him of his wife Ellen who died years ago on Stephen's Day, or maybe because he never had kids of his own. But he'd always sit alone in the kitchen on Christmas night when we'd all be in the parlour playing with our games and toys. He was a great man for the prayers though and would always go to the three masses on Christmas morning and spend hours kneeling in front of the big crib in the church with all the real hay. He lent me wood once to make our own crib. It was in the *Ireland's Own* how you could do it. I built it in the backyard and it took me four days. You had to cut out all the sides first then the roof and nail them all together. The nails in our house were never the same size and sometimes you had to straighten out some of the crooked ones so you'd have enough. I must have made a mistake with the measure-ments because when I was finished it wouldn't fit in the back door. At least our cats had a house of their own for the winter and didn't have to worry about staying with Bobby if he was in bad humour.

My ma's mother and father died in tragic circumstances. She was only thirty-three and had to go to England for a funeral but she caught pneumonia off someone over there and died soon after. Her da only lasted about two years longer and died of a broken heart when he got an injury on their farm and it turned septic. That's why Uncle Mick had to take Ma and Bridie and Chrissie and Nicky into his house when they were very small and everyone said it must have been the shock of that killed Uncle Mick's wife Ellen at an early age. So Ma and her sister Auntie Chrissie were the only ones left in the house now, with all of us and Da and maybe Uncle Mick wanted to let us have Christmas night on our own.

Even though I loved Da the best I was very fond of Uncle Mick. I knew, because he was the oldest, that he'd be the first death in our family and I overheard my ma saying that it was a sure sign of ageing when they got up at half four every morning to potter around and light the fire so I decided to keep a special eye on him. I started to get up early before anyone else and make him a cup of tea. He'd tell me loads of stories about when he was a cowboy in America and had to hunt all the cows on a big white horse that was called Paddy and that's why they gave him the job on the cattle boat in Dublin. His memory was very good and I'd watch him really carefully cutting his toast to see if he was getting a shaky hand. One morning he fell asleep sitting in front of the fire and that was my chance. I put my hands on his head to make sure he wasn't going to die soon.

But on Christmas morning when we'd all be opening our presents in the parlour beside the Christmas tree with the colourful lights flickering in the dark you'd know by his face no matter how hard he tried that he was disappointed with the same black socks so that year I persuaded Ma to make him a cardigan. She let me pick out a colour for the wool. It was bright red and Ma wasn't sure about it at all but you should have seen his face when he opened the parcel. He wore it nearly every day 'cos I'd say he was sick of the black and grey and he was so careful with it and never spilt tobacco juice on it. It was the one day of the year you were allowed stay up as late as you wanted, but no matter how hard I tried, I was still in bed at nearly the same time as always, but at least Uncle Mick was happy and wasn't going to die. I'd still kept two presents to open the next day, and even though my brother Tommy had broken my new toy saxophone, Da said he'd solder it back together when he went back to work and there hadn't even been one row in our house all day.

Tom Daly was a strange boy – the only one on our street that wasn't really from Dublin. They had moved up from Athlone to stay with the Barkers when his daddy died. Just him and his ma because he was an only child. He knew everything about horses and all that stuff because he was from the country, and whenever your cat brought in a rat or a bird he could deal with it. He was only twelve but he could even clean and stuff the turkeys in our street for Christmas when our butcher started charging all the neighbours too much because he'd won the prize bonds and didn't care about his customers any more. O'Reilly was his name and you'd be sent down there on Saturday sometimes for a pound and a half of round steak, half minced, and a bone for the dog. And Ma always warned you to make sure he'd cut the steak in half and mince it fresh, otherwise you wouldn't know what rubbish he was giving you and he hated that, specially from a small kid while he'd be chatting up all the women from the parish and getting away with murder. But once he won the money, he didn't give two fecks about anyone and I was delighted when he moved out to Blackrock. Da told Ma that we'd seen his true colours, but Bobby was a bit disappointed because whatever about the mince, he must have loved dogs and would always give you huge leftover bones.

Anyway when Tom Daly moved into our parish you'd have to love him because they were so poor. It was the summer and he was always in his bare feet. He said that's what they always do down the country and thank God nobody jeered him for that. But once the butcher closed up for good, at Christmas time there'd be a huge queue outside their house to get the turkeys done and I'd say he made a right few bob out of that. We called him Smudgie because I don't think his ma was great at getting him to wash his face and he used to deliver coal to all the neighbours on his days off the turkeys. His ma never made him go to school and some days he'd let you help him. All you had to do was sit up in the driver's seat on the horse and cart when he was carrying in the huge bags of coal, and make sure the horse didn't run away. He'd always collect jam jars and old clothes from every house and like my Aunt Chrissie he never stopped smiling with his big red country face.

He used to borrow the horse and cart off Mr Cartwright who had a farmyard at the back of our house. I knew he had to pay his rental money for the whole lot because I saw him paying over two pounds in coins one Friday evening. Mr Cartwright loved him like a son. Mr Cartwright kept greyhounds as well and used to feed them crushed sheep skulls every night, but Tom Daly only was interested in the horse and cart. The horse was called Beano and was so gentle, so it had to be a big mistake when Mr Cartwright was backing in the cart one night into the yard in the lane. He must have been standing in the wrong place because he was crushed to death in seconds. He had a huge funeral even though I don't think he had any family. But Mad Micky Tohill who lived in our street walked down the aisle of the church with his hand on the coffin as usual. He had a great funeral, four black horses with white plumes out to Glasnevin Cemetery in the Saturday rain, and hundreds from our parish went along and Da said he must have been a very loved man.

Nobody knew what to do about his horses and his greyhounds that he loved. I climbed over the back wall that night into his yard with my older brother Tommy. The corporation men had put new concrete on the road over Johnny Cullen's bridge and covered it with hay to help it dry. Tommy waited until they'd all gone home and robbed two sackfuls. I'd sat outside the new butcher's all day waiting for him to throw out all the old meat and bones. So between us the animals wouldn't starve. When we climbed over the back wall into the farmyard, we needn't have worried. There was Tom Daly in his bare feet in the moonlight, calming them all down and feeding them and Tommy told me to leave all our stuff there and get home quick because they were in great hands. When we told Da what happened, he sent me off to bed early, but I heard him tell Tommy not to worry, that God had his own way of looking after things, especially animals – and he was right. Within a week, Tom Daly owned the whole shebang, lock stock and barrel and he only twelve. Ma said he had to do it through his mother's name, and not to be getting any ideas because he had a special talent and we'd still have to go to school. But from that day on, Tom Daly was my special hero and I gave up wearing shoes for a while until Ma made me put them back on.

You always got a few bob for doing weddings when you were an altar boy. Once even a ten-shilling note. They were nearly always on Saturdays or sometimes during the week so you'd get off school. Only the boys who served the seven mass in the morning would get asked and I always put my name down for that. Mr Shelley the church clerk was brilliant at guessing if they were rich. The vestry would be full of the wedding people signing the register. He'd rub the palm of his hand off the corner of the table to let me know I'd do very well. Then I'd hang around folding up priests' vestments, making a big fuss, and bumping into them in case they'd forget about me. But they were always very generous, even the poor ones would always slip me the money in an envelope. Mr Shelley used drink in the same pub as Da and he'd put my name down for the weddings as often as he could.

Outside the rusty gates of the church when the bride and groom would be getting into the big car covered in confetti, loads of kids would be waiting around for the grush. Then, just as the cars were pulling away, the best man would throw a big bunch of coins out the car window and the kids would mill in, pushing and shoving to grab as much as they could. The altar boys weren't allowed to join in because we'd been looked after already.

One boy, Paddy Flynn, was brilliant at it. He wasn't the biggest of them but he always came out with the most. He was one of my best pals in school, but he couldn't join our gang because he was from the flats. He was very good at the lessons though and every time I was having a go at being first in the class he'd always beat me. I never saw much of him in the summer, but at four o'clock after school we'd often go down to the docks and play in the timber yard, or watch the cattle being hunted onto the ships. His da was a sailor and that's what he was going to be when he grew up. He was going to join the Irish Merchant Navy and be a captain. He had a small silver compass in his pocket and he'd get me to help him practise treasure maps. I just had to hide a penny somewhere in the timber yard and mark out how many steps north-north-west and the ninety-degree turn for another good few steps. He was very good at it and I knew it wouldn't take him long being a captain, once he got going. His da used to be away for months, all over the world. I think he missed him a lot.

One day he asked me to do a special favour and not tell anyone about it. His da was coming home suddenly next week and his ma was in big trouble. They had two huge bronze statues of Buddha in the house that his da brought home from Singapore. Every time he was coming home they'd have to be shined up spotless with Brasso. But this time when the da was away his ma'd got stuck for money and got their uncle to bring them up to the pawnshop that my ma never went to, in his car. There must have been a big family misfortune because the uncle had to sell the car, that's what Paddy Flynn said although they never told him exactly what the misfortune was. But no matter what happened the Buddhas had to be got back before the da came home. She'd borrowed off a moneylender to be able to get them back. He seemed a bit shy telling me all this and I swore I wouldn't tell a soul. Anyway he said da always came home with loads of money and his ma could pay the moneylender straight back. His problem was they were so heavy he couldn't carry them on his own. So of course I said I'd help. He took the bunch of money out of his pocket, all pound notes. Then we both had the brilliant idea at exactly the same time.

His ma didn't want us to go near the pawnshop until nearly closing time when there wouldn't be too many people around so we had hours to spare. We made out treasure maps and it was my turn to be the finder. I closed my eyes up to a hundred. Then he handed me the map and sat down laughing 'cos I was so bad at it and wasn't even getting warm. I was half an hour searching until he got fed up.

'Here Robbie, you're thick. C'mon I'll show you.' He started pacing out − forward − left forward − right − right. I knew by the look on his face it was a disaster. He went back to the start and began again. His face was white and we both started panicking. We pulled the big timber planks backwards and forwards − nothing. He sat down and started crying. I had another go but it was useless. All the Buddhas' money had completely disappeared and there wasn't even any wind. We said a prayer to Saint Anthony − but that wasn't much use either. We were pulling whole racks of wood all over the place when a man drove in with a fork-lift and spotted us. 'Get the fuck out of there you pair of bollixes.' He jumped off and started running towards us. He was only about ten yards away when Paddy screamed, 'I found it! I found it!' The man was fast but we were hopping like mad between the timber and got out the gate. We raced down Castle Forbes Road and didn't stop till we got near our church. Paddy Flynn insisted we go in and light a candle in front of Saint Anthony's statue and we did.

There was no more messing now and we went straight to the pawn. I was never in there before. It was a huge place, mainly bundles of clothes tied up with white sheets and little tags. Paddy Flynn told me they kept all the precious goods out the back. Mr O'Farrell was on duty. He had a bald head and didn't look a bit like Kevin. He pretended he didn't recognise me, or maybe he was blind. He took a long look at the docket, the money and us. Then he nodded his head and went in the back. We could hear him puffing and panting before we saw him, and even then it was hard to because the Buddhas were so huge. Paddy Flynn looked at me and I looked at him and we both knew our troubles were only starting. If you gripped it right you could get nearly ten steps before stopping for a rest. I'd never seen a Buddha before. They're very fat with a smiley face, but this wasn't funny. We started trying to break the record and go for twenty steps. Paddy Flynn was a bit smaller than me but much stronger and once he got to twenty-four, even though I had very strong hands from Bobby pulling the lead.

After an hour and a bit we were halfway home. Paddy Flynn said we could take a break because he wanted to have a smoke. We sat down on the kerb and a lot of people stopped to have a look at us. Paddy Flynn pulled out his fags and didn't his lovely silver compass fall out of his pocket and roll down the shore. 'Ah Jaysus no.' He was like Da, he hardly ever cursed. It was easy enough to pull up the grating but it was completely full of muck. He was in it up to his elbow then his armpit because it was very deep. My arms were longer than his so I had a go. We pulled up bits of stone, a steel marble, even a penny coin – everything was covered in slime and the smell was rotten eggs. Finally we got it and did our best to clean it. It seemed to be working OK. The sooner we got home the better so off we started. It was very hard to hold onto the Buddhas now because our hands were all muck. At least it was getting dark and there weren't too many people around to jeer at us and make stupid jokes. The worst part was getting them up the steps in the flats because they lived in the fourth balcony. I never saw anyone like Paddy Flynn. It was definitely his prayers that made every-thing work out. And here he was now taking turns carrying both of the big bronze smiling Buddhas up the steps to the flats because I was too bollixed. He just wouldn't give up and let his ma or da down. The Buddhas took up most of the space in their tiny sitting room. The ma was delighted that they weren't scratched. She wiped off the muck in seconds and made me stay for tea. His three younger sisters were sitting at the table drawing 'Welcome Home' cards for their da. Mrs Flynn didn't seem to mind when Paddy sat back in the armchair and lit up a cigarette. I wondered was it too late for my da to become a sailor.

Da was staying in my room that night because it was Lent. Everyone else was asleep so we had a great chat. I told him all about my adventure that day but never mentioned who it was. I told Da I'd promised to keep the secret and he said that was gameball, but there was no way he was going to become a sailor because he couldn't even look at the ferry crossing the Liffey without feeling seasick and anyway he was too old. But I could if I wanted to because it was a fine job, and to remember I was born with a caul and couldn't drown and Mr Brown on our street was a ship's captain. He was always in fine fettle and must be making loads of money because they'd bought the house off Mrs Hobson and were always doing it up. Da didn't think I'd make a motor mechanic because I didn't seem to have much patience. Then I went through the whole lot with him. Maybe a carpenter or a hypnotist or a faith healer, but definitely not a priest. He said there was good money in the carpentry but wasn't sure about the other stuff and I should take my time. There wasn't any hurry and he'd look after me until I was old enough to make up my own mind.

Then I told him my big worry about school, about poxy Finch and having to do everything through Irish, even geometry and Latin, and that they certainly weren't the happiest days of my life. Then he told me something he hadn't told any of us before. When he was thirteen he was in a Christian Brother school. He was very quiet and shy but loved writing English. One day the Brother they nicknamed Galway, because that's where he was from, was writing on the board and heard someone messing. He turned and threw the wooden duster and it hit Da on the face right between the eyes. Da just got up quietly and took his schoolbag and walked out of the class and never went back. His da stood by him and he got a job as an apprentice in a garage. But he often thought if that day had never happened, he would have gone on to be a teacher because that's what he always wanted.

The light was out in the bedroom but I knew by his voice that he was really sad. I didn't say anything for a while. I could hear the bells of Christchurch in the distance, tolling out the midnight hour. The wind was rattling the windowpanes. But all I could think of was how great a teacher Da would have been, with his great stories and his gentleness. Before I could say anything I heard Da's voice, very quietly. 'Robbie, don't let anyone stop you doing what you want to do. Not me, not Ma, not anyone.' His voice was so quiet I was afraid he was going to cry so I got him to tell me again the story about how him and Ma met, about what he wore on his wedding day, about him walking home from Howth when he was a kid and all his money was gone and about him racing in the Grand Prix in Phoenix Park and nearly finishing third.

He was back in good humour again so I took a chance and asked him what happened his brother Mossy. Da said he was a little bit tired but would tell me another day, and to say my prayers and a special one for his brother Mossy. I said mine and I could hear him muttering Hail Mary, Holy Mary, until he fell asleep. Everything was quiet in the house now. Just a dog in the distance giving the odd bark. The light from the lamp-post outside Barrett's house shone across the room and I could see Da's sleeping face. He looked so peaceful he must have been having happy dreams. I hoped his brother Mossy was having them too.

I loved Easter but I hated Lent. Once Good Friday came along I was happy enough, because that was the busiest time for an altar boy, and you were put in charge of all the others, and could carry the big gold crucifix right through the church down the aisles and stop at all the stations of the cross and think how soon Easter would be. You could start eating sweets again, especially the macaroon bars that you bought every week in Darcy's shop during Lent and hid them in the coal scuttle in the parlour because it was never used until Christmas. But the Corpus Christi processions were the best. In the middle of summer, June I think, with all the streets and avenues and the flats in our parish decked out with flags and bunting in crimson, yellow, gold and red, all glistening in the sun. You'd be at the front with the big gold crucifix and right behind you the Blessed Sacrament in a white monstrance with gold rays carried by the priest in white vestments trimmed with orange, covered by a violet canopy carried by the men from the Sacred Heart conference in their deep blue robes, and then the army right behind with their guns held high in salute to the body of Christ. Behind them came all the girls in their white communion dresses and the boys in their new suits with the red rosettes. Then the Lawrence O'Toole's pipe band in their black and amber uniforms, just beating the drums, and after them anyone else that wanted to walk along.

The people in the flats had the best altars outside, their houses drenched with tulips of all the colours in the rainbow and lilac and it hardly ever rained. But at high mass at midnight on Easter, all the priests would be in their gold vestments to celebrate the Resurrection of Christ. Every few steps they'd stop and chant in Latin 'Deo Gratias' and we'd all answer 'Ora Pro Nobis'. It took nearly two hours but you'd be so intoxicated by the sound of the Latin, and the spicy scent of the incense, that you'd soon forget that there was nearly six weeks of sweets and chocolate that you'd bought but never eaten until this great Sunday.

When you'd get up early on Easter Sunday morning, Uncle Mick would already be in his best suit for first mass and he'd always tell you that he'd seen the sun dancing because that was a country tradition. Lent was horrible though. It started off not too bad on Pancake Tuesday when you could eat as much of them as you wanted with sugar and lemon until you nearly got sick. Tommy broke the world record one year when he ate twenty-three and would have kept going only Ma ran out of flour. The next day, Ash Wednesday, you had to go to church and get the cross of ashes on your forehead and the priest warned you that you would end up as dust. Da would always promise Ma he'd given up drink for Lent but it never lasted more than two days. No matter how early you got up on Ash Wednesday, Da would always have his cross of ashes already on him, once even before the church was open. I think Tommy copped on as well because I caught him one Ash Wednesday putting his finger into the grate because he was late for school.

I never noticed Tommy giving up anything. He said he did his own thing, but me and Shea were forced to give up sweets and crisps and nearly everything except chewing gum didn't count because it was good for your teeth.

Shea was a little squirrel and he never cheated once, not even on St Patrick's Day. I don't know how he did it but the minute he got his pocket money on Friday he'd be straight down to the shop and buy as many honey bees and circus toffees that he could and pile them up in the left side of the coal scuttle. Nearly every night he'd count them up. He had a notebook and wrote everything down so no one could steal anything. I never knew what Da gave up but he was always sent into our bedroom to sleep during Lent. I loved it, it was the only good thing about Lent and he'd tell us loads of stories about a witch called Spikser who lived near them in St Anne's Park when he was younger.

He certainly never gave up the drink though. In fact, I thought he drank more than ever during Lent and some nights he could be terrible grumpy, especially if you stood on his feet getting into bed.

Mr Cartwright was a lovely man before his tragic death when his horse and cart crushed him. Before Tom Daly arrived he used to let me help him when he came back in the evenings after delivering stuff all over the place.

My job was to crush the sheep skulls with an iron bar and feed them to the greyhounds, but he'd never let me near his two horses that had to be washed every night and fed warm bran from a steel bucket. He loved those horses and would shine and polish up their bridles and things every single night. On Saturday nights him and my Uncle Nicky would take a greyhound down to Shelbourne Park for the races. He always said to me that one day he'd have a Derby winner. There was one greyhound that he was sure would do it for him. It was white with black spots so he was called Spotty, but you had to give them a racing name so he was called Wicklow Express even though he was born in Wexford. I wasn't very fond of him because one day he tried to climb over our backyard to eat Bobby. And if you went near him when he was eating the sheep skulls he'd take the hand off you.

There was a big race on one Saturday night and he couldn't get Uncle Nicky out of the pub so he asked me to give him a hand. We walked all the way there. He had to sign him in and get him weighed so we were very early. He left me holding the dog behind the stand because he'd met some of his friends from the country and wanted to have a drink with them. Then a lot of other men came along with dogs and asked me to hold onto them as well. They must have thought I was working for the place. I ended up with about six dogs.

They were quiet enough at first. Then the bell rang for the first race and they started to go mad. I did my very best but no matter how strong I was from walking Bobby on the lead, I could barely hold onto them and they even started trying to bite each other. All the leads were getting tangled, so it was lucky they were all muzzled. Some of the men came back and called me all sorts of a fucking eejit and never gave me a tip. Finally, thank God, I was just left with Wicklow Express. I knew it was getting very near the time for our race but there was no sign of Mr Cartwright. Then the loudspeaker called out a list of dogs and Spotty was in trap six. I panicked and ran around to where the bar was. I think it was the first time the betters ever saw a greyhound in there.

Spotty took a few nips at anyone near him and they all started looking up their racing cards. I heard one man saying that feckin' thing has no chance, then Mr Cartwright came running down. He patted me on the head and apologised and we went straight down onto the track. They put a black-and-white-striped number six on Spotty and a white coat on me. I had to walk around the track with him and keep him in the queue with the other dogs. Mr Cartwright asked me did Spotty have a shit. When I nodded he just said, 'Good man,' as if I'd done it myself, and he ran straight to the bookies.

I didn't know but you had to put your dog in the trap all by yourself. Spotty went in backwards and slowed the whole thing down. Everyone was giving out hell until the man with the number one dog came over and gave me a hand. I didn't realise that you had to catch them as well after the race but he said he'd help me out, and just to follow him. He said Spotty looked frisky enough and he liked the cut of his jib.

After the race, and after Spotty won by a mile all the dogs were trying to eat each other and the hare, but the number one dog man helped me get Spotty back on his lead. On our way home Mr Cartwright gave me a ten-shilling note and said it was a great idea bringing the dog into the bar because he went off at a great price. Me and Spotty had to wait outside Mulligan's pub in Poolbeg Street while Mr Cartwright had his Guinness with his friends. I was delighted with the ten bob. But back in the yard I told Mr Cartwright that I didn't really want to do that again. Afterwards when Mr Cartwright died in the tragic accident, Spotty and the other greyhounds were sent down the country to a good home.

That was only the second time ever I was left standing outside a pub. The other time was when Da finally met his brother Mossy – the black sheep. A man from Da's pub told him he'd seen him coming out of the lveagh Hostel. I used to go over there so many times to the baths, you'd think I would have spotted him immediately, so he mustn't look a bit like Da. The man from Da's pub used to work on the railways like Uncle Mossy who was a train driver, but had lost touch with him over the years. So the minute he saw him he recognised him. They'd gone for a chat over a cup of tea and the man finally realised that the favourite brother he was talking about was Da. Da didn't hesitate for a second. He made up a bundle of clothes including his two best suits. Ma said he was very foolish and the whole thing was probably a big mistake. But I went over there with Da that night and saw how disappointed he was when the man told Da that Uncle Mossy had moved on weeks ago. Da didn't know what to do but he left the clothes in for Uncle Mossy just in case he came back. He wrote a little letter and left it in one of the pockets just in case.

On the way home that night Da finally told me nearly everything about him. They were best pals as brothers and hardly ever had a row. Uncle Mossy was a year older than Da but always looked after him. When they were caught robbing orchards, he'd take the blame. They used to walk out to dances in Howth together and all the way back singing rebel songs, and he was brilliant on the violin. He was a great goalie in hurling as well. He was very fond of the girls though and was always getting into trouble. He sounded so like me that when me and Da were walking down the Boundary Wall, I made a vow that I'd never fight with Shea again in case either of us became a black sheep.

When we got home Ma wanted to hear all the news and she let me listen. That's when I learned that he got married about the same time as Ma and Da. A lovely girl from Finglas. They had loads of babies really quick, about four. But he was a martyr for the drink and one day he let the new baby fall and the wife threw him out. That was the night I swore I'd never take it up.

The last time Da met him years ago he was down on his uppers. Da brought him back to our house. Ma was very fond of him but she always thought he had a black cloud over him. I barely remember him because I was only about five. It was only a few days before Christmas, but he was allowed take his kids out with him for just one day. They were cousins I'd never really seen before. You could see he was really mad about them and they loved him. He'd brought them all to Clery's and bought them all huge Christmas presents. I was raging with Da because he never became a black sheep, but Uncle Mossy got his son a brand new bicycle with gears and a proper light and they were allowed eat all our chocolate biscuits for Christmas and we couldn't eat any. Da put a bottle of Guinness up for him but he wouldn't drink it in front of his kids.

I remember even back then that he didn't look a bit like Da. He was smaller and looked a lot older but he had the same kind eyes. You could see his shoes needed a good polish. He made a big fuss over us all but Ma wouldn't let us take any money off him. That was the last time Da saw him until one night we were on our way home from our walk with Bobby, and Da saw him walking into Bertie Donelly's pub. So when he asked me to wait outside I didn't care how long it would take.

It was a Sunday evening and there wasn't much traffic. Me and Bobby sat on the kerb. I was counting all the coloured marbles I'd swapped that day. Da would always bring us home huge steel ones from the ball bearings off trucks they had to fix in the garage and you'd get great swaps for those. I was hoping Da would bring Uncle Mossy home to live with us. He could sleep with Uncle Mick and it would be much better for him than with strangers in a hostel.

I decided then and there that I'd definitely never touch a drop of drink in my life, not even a sip out of Da's glass of Guinness because it must run in the family and when I got married I'd hate to be thrown out and have to live somewhere else. I peeped in the window once after about an hour. I had to stand on the ledge and climb up onto the window sill because the window was nearly all stained glass. They were chatting away inside getting on great. Uncle Mossy was laughing like mad, but I wouldn't say he was playing hurling any more because he looked very old. But the great thing was he was wearing one of Da's good suits.

I was dying to have a pee now but I didn't want to go in and disturb them. I went down the lane beside the new butcher's shop that Ma really liked. Mr Cuddy was locking up but when he saw us he went back in and got a big bone for Bobby. I saw Clicky Kelly's gang passing by the end of the lane. So I stayed there for a while in case they'd try to steal my coloured marbles. Then I walked up to the bridge where me and Da would watch the trains shunting. It would be great if Uncle Mossy still had that job. Maybe he really would come and live with us and let me sit in the cabin when he was driving the train to Limerick.

We went back to the pub. I sat on the kerb again and took a pencil out of my top jacket pocket and a bit of Belvedere Bond paper that I always carried with me. I drew a map of Ireland. I knew where Wexford was, and Kerry. I was sure Belfast was up by the teddy-bear's head.

But I really wanted to go to Limerick where Ma and Da had their honeymoon and I hoped it would be a long way away, because I wanted Uncle Mossy to let me drive a little bit of the way.

It was getting cold now and very dark, Bobby had finished his bone and was whining to go home. I climbed back up to look in the pub window. They were gone! Even though Uncle Mossy didn't look a bit like Da, they had exactly the same voice and laugh. I could hear them before I even knocked at the door of 11 Emerald Street. Shea let me in, shouting, 'Uncle Mossy is here! Uncle Mossy is here!' There they all were in the kitchen having a great time. Uncle Mossy and Da drinking their bottles of Guinness, Ma handing out the ham sandwiches and biscuits and all my brothers and sisters laughing and eating away like mad. I was glad Da had found his brother but I couldn't believe he'd forgotten about me and I'd never forgive him for that. Maybe I was being mean, but that night I was hoping Uncle Mossy would go home to his own family.

The Jesuits were the best laugh when you were an altar boy. They'd come in to the parish for two weeks every year to do the missions and call into all the houses to put everyone back on the right road and get them to go to lectures every single night at eight o'clock, one week for the men and one week for the women. Da said they were holy terrors the way they'd put the fear of God in you about hell. They were always going on about the ninth commandment, Thou shalt not covet thy neighbour's wife, but Da said if they took a good look at the other wives on our street they'd have to pay him to covet them and wasn't he lucky he was married to Ma. And anyway wasn't there only two real commandments – Love God and Love thy neighbour, and he found the second one the hardest but he'd always do his best.

46

But there was no way Ma could get Da to go to the missions. Even though the Jesuits would go down to all the pubs and hunt the men out into the church, Da would never drink in Noctor's that week and the pub up in Amiens Street would have a bumper week with all the men. None of us altar boys were allowed listen in to the lectures about sins of the flesh, so you got a good few nights off before you had to come back for the benedictions. Mad Micky Tohill never missed a night even for the women's week. Nobody minded and he had his own chorus for all the Latin hymns.

You were allowed play relievio on sins of the flesh night and on the women's week there'd be no Ma around to give out to you so you could run and hide all over the parish even in the Sheriff Street flats, where the other team would never find you hiding on the fourth balcony, but you had to be back in the vestry by nine. Jimmy Jackson used to sweat a lot and after all the running there'd be a terrible smell off his feet if you had to kneel beside him on the altar but not if you were swinging the thurible because there was such a lovely smell off the incense. He hardly ever washed so I set a trap for him one night. I saw him talking outside the convent to two girls and knew he'd be next in so I balanced a big bucket of water on top of the half-open vestry door – at least it would cool him down a bit and take away some of the smell. I was sitting inside waiting and laughing when in walked one of the Jesuits and got the shock and the drowning of his life. Before he even looked around I was up the stairs and out on the altar lighting all the candles even though it wasn't my job. He came straight out onto the altar looking for the culprit so I hid behind the huge pulpit. He was dripping wet with his red face and I knew the women were in for a terrible time that night. I was afraid to move so had to sit there all night, and even though I hadn't a clue what he was on about, he was ripping every woman apart, starting with Eve and the Whores of Babylon, not forgetting Lot's wife, Jezebel and Mary Magdalene and I wet myself for the first time in years.

Kevin O'Farrell's family were very religious. He had seven older sisters and they were all in the Legion of Mary. Everyone expected Kevin to become a priest. They had a lovely big house right across the street from our church and the priests were always popping in and out for cups of tea. Their da owned the pawnshop in our parish that Ma would never go to. All his customers called him Uncle Tommy so that must have been his name. Their ma was a lovely woman and would always invite me in for a big fry.

One day we were chatting in their big sitting room with all the lovely furniture. Everyone was out, just me and Kevin. It was the day before Ash Wednesday so we were eating the last of a big box of chocolate biscuits and talking about what we were giving up for Lent. Kevin said he wasn't giving up anything but was going to go to mass every morning and benediction every night, and give up the sinning till Easter Sunday. Then he told me his secret. He had decided to become a Franciscan as soon as they'd let him and spend his whole life in Africa saving souls. He'd already joined their Third Order. He brought me up to his bedroom to show me something. He had a room all to himself with a coloured eiderdown, and no coats on his bed. Underneath it he pulled out a case and showed me what was inside. It was a lovely brown habit with a white rope around the middle with a hood. He put it over his clothes and it fitted him perfectly. I could just imagine him older with a big red beard and sandals walking through the jungle, loads of people following. Just like Jesus. I had to get one straight away – all you had to do was join the

Third Order and go to their chapel in Church Street every Thursday night. If you missed even one night you wouldn't get it, and would have to start all over again. If you died tragically in childhood in an accident they'd allow you to get buried in it and say a high mass for you with all their monks standing around your coffin. Ma was delighted I'd taken up the religion again, but I said nothing to her about the habit. I wanted to surprise her.

The first Thursday I went there everyone except the new people like me were wearing the brown skirts. They knew the words of all the hymns as well. Because it was Lent, they had the Jesuits in to give the sermon. I spotted the one I'd dropped the bucket of water on. The church was packed so I kept my head down in my hands and pretended to be praying hard all the time, in case he spotted me. They were doing the sins of the flesh, one for men, but we were allowed to stay this time. I didn't understand most of it but it must have been working because a lot of the men around me were sweating. Then a terrible thing happened. A man sitting in the seat in front of me in his ordinary clothes – he must have been a beginner like me – started moaning and swaying in the seat. He was so close I could see the dandruff on the back of his head and the sweat running down his neck. The priest was roaring about how long eternity in the fires of hell would last. If you took only just one grain of sand off Dollymount beach every year until the beach was clear, that wouldn't even add up to your first second in the unquenchable fires that were so hot they'd melt the fillings in your teeth, whilst the evilest snakes you could imagine would devour any part of your body that you'd sinned with, and you'd never see the face of God.

I was just thinking to myself that not seeing the face of God would be the least of your worries, when the man in front of me jumped to his feet shouting, 'Jaysus – Jaysus

– Enough! That's enough!' He ran straight down the aisle roaring curses and frightened the life out of everyone. But the priest never stopped for a second. The fires in hell were getting hotter and eternity was getting longer. I looked across at Kevin's face and hoped he'd stick with the Franciscans and not go near the Jesuits. I couldn't imagine the souls in Africa putting up with this kind of stuff because it was hot enough out there already. A few more beginner men snook out quietly but I was determined to get my habit so I stuck it till the end.

After the whole thing was over there was huge crowds for confession. I couldn't remember any sins so I didn't bother. Me and Kevin walked home together, but I couldn't get a word out of him. He was white in the face. He'd put the habit back in the brown suitcase that he'd carried with him and his hands were shaking. Then a funny thing happened as we were standing at the traffic lights in Amiens Street. He handed me the suitcase and told me I could keep it forever. He'd changed his mind about the whole priest thing and was going to go into business with his da when he finished school. I didn't try to talk him out of it. I was just delighted I had my own habit without ever having to go back near any of them again. The next week when everyone was asleep in the middle of the night, I'd get up and put on my habit and practise being a monk. There was a big Pascal candle in our house from last Easter and I'd light it up and walk up and down the hall in the pitch dark in my bare feet in the habit, chanting bits of Latin that I'd remembered from being an altar boy at funerals.

One night Da must have been doing overtime because he didn't come in until really late. I didn't hear his key in the latch because he was trying to be very quiet and I frightened the bejaysus out of him. It was only the second time I ever heard him curse. He slammed the hall door fast and stayed outside coughing for nearly ten minutes. I knew I was in big trouble, so I ran up to bed and hid everything away. It was Lent so he was staying in our room. I pretended to be asleep and not hear him when he finally came in. He never said a word but knelt down beside the bed and started muttering prayers to Jesus, and especially to Saint Francis, and loads of promises about how he'd give up the drink and take the pledge. It lasted a good few weeks but I wasn't happy about it at all. He'd be home early every night and was the first one to pull out the rosary beads once all our ecker was done. Ma was delighted of course, but he was terrible cranky. I heard Ma telling her friend Theresa that he'd become very hard to live with since he'd seen his vision. Theresa said it was probably the horrors, whatever that was, and it probably wouldn't last.

Theresa was right. A few weeks later, I heard a huge row going on in our bedroom. I opened the door a tiny bit, and saw Da holding up my habit in front of Tommy and taking a few swipes at him. Then he burst out the door and shouted into the kitchen to Ma that he was going for a few feckin' pints. Tommy hadn't a clue what was going on, but the damage was done so there was no point in saying a word. But Ma was back in charge of starting the rosary again and Da had stopped threatening to get the whole house exorcised. The next day I brought Kevin's brown case with the habit in it up to the canal bridge and threw it in. I watched it sink slowly and wondered would Kevin with all those sisters ever really become a priest. At least things were back to normal again in our house and Da gave me his lovely white pioneer pin with the red picture of the Sacred Heart.

It was St Patrick's Day and even the sun was cold. But no matter what Ma said I wouldn't wear a coat, because

I wanted to show off my green tweed jacket with the harp and the Fairview Park clover all pinned high on the left side – the men's side – and I hoped the American visitors wouldn't notice the four leaves. I stood near the GPO, the best place to watch the American cheerleaders with their short skirts and lovely tanned legs high-kicking to the music. I tried hard not to stare at their knickers and nearly succeeded. This was my favourite day and I didn't want to mess it up with a sin of bad thoughts. The parade was over too fast and my knees were raw cold as I turned into the freezing wind coming up from the docks. Everyone played football in Emerald Street now in their Patrick's Day best. My black expensive confirmation shoes had lasted longer than usual but were nearly banjaxed now with all the scrapes of stones and kerbs and street dirt and I'd have to hide them from Ma, far in under the bed with the picture of the topless lady that I'd stolen from Aunt Chrissie's medical book.

The dinner on Patrick's Day was always better than Sundays with roast beef, jelly and ice cream and you were allowed not to eat the smelly cabbage. Uncle Mick gave us a full shilling as me and Shea headed for Croker with my best pal Kevin O'Farrell and a few others, even David Casey because I was beginning to hope when we called for him that his sister Marian, that was nearly my girl-friend once, might be wearing one of them cheerleader's short skirts.

On the way to Croker we didn't see Apple Annie with her cider bottle hiding under the arches until she leapt out and grabbed me and dragged my face close to hers. I could feel the spits as she cursed me for no reason. Kevin said gypsies like her had the power and it was a very bad luck thing and wanted to go home. Outside Croker there was a huge crowd. We shoved our way along the inside wall up to the schoolboys' gate. It wasn't easy because all the country men were there shoving and shouting and fatter than Da.

''Tis a disgrace – why don't ye open more stiles!' Then there was a massive roar from inside. Someone must have scored a goal.

'Christ, we'll miss the whole feckin' thing, come on lads – let's burst the gates open!'

Loads of men were shouting. They started to ram the gates. It was a terrible crush but I squeezed along towards the men's gate thinking I could get in free and save the shilling for the pictures. I couldn't see Shea or the others anywhere. Suddenly my face was right up against the big green gate. The crush was really bad now. I couldn't get my hand that was holding the shilling out of my pocket. The gates were bending, another big push, they gave a bit more, then another, then crack! the lock snapped, the gates swung back, a mad rush and roar.

'Hold on – move back!' Some people fall. A woman right in front of me falls forward – my foot is on her back.

'Get off my back – get off my back!' she screams. I just can't help it. I try to lift it. My other foot gets caught. Too late – I'm down – my face pressed hard against the woman on the ground. It's hurting now. Can hardly breathe. I try to turn my head around. It suddenly goes dark. There must be four or five on top. I try to shout for help – no sound. My mouth pressed deeper now. I can't breathe. I cannot breathe. No prayers. Just the thought, 'I'm goin' – I'm gonna die. I'm much too young – ah God I've only just begun.' No feeling in my hands. My head won't turn. The roaring in my ears. 'I'm gonna die! Ah Ma – please Da. A prayer – say it quick – no time – I want to live – I want to live – I want – Jesus on your cross – do not forsake me! Is this – is this the end?'

Like a dream now. Calm now, along the beach – the sun is white and strong and warm. The waves roll smooth, so calm. The sound laps soft then soft then strong, so soft and strong but steady like the beat, the pulse, the pulse warm pulse, the waves lap louder now, and stronger so strong, the breathing with the waves grows strong, the sounds much closer now, each rush of wave and ebb much closer than the last, the water rolls across my face and leaves me clean and warm and closer now, the sound, my breath starts deep and rushes with the waves, gasp deep and breathe again, make a resurrection with each calming breath, so clean so free and sounds begin to come right in, and now some thoughts of where I am, no sight but still alive. A man shouts in my ears as if I wasn't there. I smile a lazy freedom smile. No pressure now, with feeling in my hands. Too tired to open up my eyes. I'm carried now by one strong man. So safe. A woollen coat against my face. A light begins to glow – can't focus on the curious shadowed faces staring down. My saviour puts his coat beneath my head and holds my hand and smiles. 'Thanks, mister, thanks,' I try to say. The man leans close to hear my voice. 'Thanks, mister, thanks – thanks for this second chance.' A promise made to keep, safe to fall asleep.

It was very quiet in the ward. The two doctors were whispering but I heard every word. There was blood coming from my eyes and my ears. They were planning to operate on my head that night. I pretended I couldn't hear anything and tried not to smile. I knew they were wrong. I'd easy cure myself. So I decided to stay awake all that night in case they tried anything on. But I must have dozed off. It was the crinkling of the packet of crisps that woke me. My da was putting them on my locker and right beside them a brand new Hohner harmonica. I didn't want to pretend I was better straight away so I lay there very still. I could feel him pushing the hair back from my forehead – the first time I ever remember him touching me. He sat down beside the bed with his big hand resting on the blanket. It was scrubbed clean but still a bit grease-stained. I wanted to touch it but couldn't. When he was lighting his cigarette I chanced a peep at him. He looked so worried I decided I'd let him know I was still alive.

'How's the others, Da?'

'All gameball.' It took him ages to do it but finally he held my hand. 'We thought we'd lost you, son.'

I opened my eyes then and knew by the look on his face that they must have been still full of blood.

'Who won the match, Da?'

'Dublin of course. Don't talk too much, son. Go back asleep.'

I couldn't tell him about the doctors' secret plan so I pretended to go fast asleep. I woke up to a huge bustle of action. Flip it – they were ready to cut open my head, but it was just my ma and my auntie sorting out my locker. I kept my eyes closed and knew exactly what my ma would say. 'Chrissie, would you just look at them underpants and I left him out a clean pair this morning.'

'Hey Ma.' I opened my eyes.

'My God, son. What happened your eyes?'

'I was bleeding from them and my ears too!'

'Well he's in the right place, Molly,' Chrissie said. I could never understand why all the older people – even my da – called her Molly when her real name was Mary. Ma said, 'Anyway, here, put these on.' She handed me pyjamas.

'I'm not wearing them!' I could tell by the smell – they were Shea's!

I'd cured myself so well I was up running around the next morning helping the nuns with the breakfasts. To tell the truth it was mainly so they wouldn't notice me not eating the lumpy porridge and the runny egg. I'd swapped them with the big man in the next bed for his toast. He was a culchie but at least he wasn't from Meath and he let me read the bit in the paper about the crush in Croke Park, with a list of the injured, and there – in print – my name and my magical address. I knew most of the lads on the street would be jealous and wished they'd got crushed and I hoped Hattie Hobson was raging she'd given me up. I got my own back on Tommy when he came in to see me. I knew there was a big sin nearly all older boys did, but you had to be at least fourteen and a half before you could try it.

'It was like dying, Tommy, I swear. Everything went dark and then very suddenly I could see this white light and it got bigger and brighter and suddenly I was there.'

'Where?' asked Tommy.

'In Heaven. And then everything became clear to me, and . . . I swear, Tommy, I could see him.'

'Who?'

'God!'

'Really?'

'Yeah.'

'Did you really see him?'

I had Tommy by the balls now. 'It was like . . .' I lay back and closed my eyes. 'It was like . . . It wasn't like those pictures with the big beard and everything. And He told me about what everyone was doing wrong.'

'But was the voice old?'

'I told you – it wasn't. Well yeah. It was like really old and booming and oh yeah – the very last thing he said was in Latin. *Ab Tomas pecatus penus.*'

'What does that mean?' Tommy whispered in awe.

'Warn Tommy to stop wanking.'

It was a great place to practise the miracles. I must have cured about seven people in that ward because they were all gone home before the end of the week. My hardest job was an old man that could barely breathe. You had to lean right over him to hear what he was saying. The staff nurse said it was emphysema or something like that. I'd never heard of it before. They were real mean to him 'cos he was always asking for a cigarette and they'd never give him one. One day I robbed a fag and a box of matches off the fat man from the country when he wasn't looking. You should have seen the old man's face light up when I sneaked them into his locker. I woke up that night and could hear a priest muttering in Latin. The nuns must have pulled the curtains around his bed, and I knew they were giving him extreme unction. I'd have to work fast. As soon as they all left I went inside the screens and put my hand on his head. He opened his eyes and smiled and fell back asleep. It was my best ever cure because when I woke up next morning the screens weren't there any more, his bed was empty and all his stuff was gone. He must have escaped during the night. At least wherever he was he could have a decent smoke now without anyone bothering him. I was thrilled but decided not to tell anyone. If they found out they'd keep me in here forever fixing people, and I was beginning to miss my dog Bobby.

I was only a week away in the Mater Hospital but our house seemed much smaller. Even Tommy sitting in the corner listening to Radio Luxembourg with his science book on his knee didn't look so big any more. Bobby lay panting in front of the kitchen fire. Da was reading the sports page in the *Irish Press*. Tipperary must have won because he had a big smile on his face. I could hear Elaine practising the piano in the parlour; only the scales but she was definitely getting better. Shea was playing cards with Mary Joe on the other side of the table and for once they weren't fighting and Uncle Mick was snoring in his chair.

I had a really happy feeling in my head as I remembered St Patrick's Day and the white light and the real voice I had heard. So clear. 'Just be fearless, and believe you can do anything, and you can.' I was smiling away to myself. No fear of Brother Finch now; God must never have spoke to him. But first things first. Some money for Ma, she was searching everywhere for a shilling for the gas. I picked up Da's *Irish Press*, found the 'Spot the Ball' picture competition, marked the 'X' and wrote the magical address. Outside the rain had stopped and Bobby waited while I said a special prayer. Between my hands I carried the envelope like a secret treasure.

I knew by the huge grin on Da's face that we'd won the hundred pounds. He never even went into the pub as he rushed home with the paper. Lucky I'd put my ma's name on the coupon 'cos kids weren't allowed enter and even Da might have been tempted by a big cheque like that. All my aunties and uncles and cousins came to the party, and the way my ma was slipping her sisters the money I knew it wouldn't last long. But it was a great night and the first time we ever used the parlour outside of Christmas. My da was playing the piano and everyone was drinking Guinness and shouting for a noble call. I never heard Ma singing before and she wasn't bad. 'The Spinning Wheel' or something with an awful lot of verses. At least there was enough money left over to buy me long trousers and pay for Tommy's scholarship books. And I heard my da tell Uncle Mick that the missus had given him ten quid for himself out of the winnings. Later that night in bed we could still hear them all singing, but the verses were shorter and seemed to be getting louder. I was feeling sick – I should never have eaten so many cakes and I wondered how long Da's money would last. Two weeks later on our Sunday-night walk I knew it was all gone. Me and Da were standing outside the Savoy cinema – *The Ten Commandments* was on. It was cold but I was wearing my longers and couldn't feel a thing. I didn't want to ask him but he saw me staring at the picture of the seas splitting open.

'Sorry son, I've hardly a make.' He produced a brown threepenny bit. Suddenly I knew exactly what to do. I grabbed the threepence.

'Wait there, Da.' I was inside the amusement arcade in a second. The man in the money desk gave me three single coppers. I knew for certain it would be the last one that'd work and watched the silver crane inside the glass case head straight for the ten-bob note wrapped inside the cream plastic ring. I nearly got knocked down twice running across O'Connell Street. The picture was great and Da had a right good few drinks in Madigan's while he waited for me and we made a deal never to tell Ma. I think that was the first time Da suspected that maybe I really could do anything.

I think poxy Finch suspected the same. He'd only ever ask kids a question if he thought they wouldn't know the answer. My first day back at school after the head thing he was doing the triangles stuff on the blackboard. It was the tricky one about the hypotenuse thing and I knew he'd lost it because he kept glancing at the clock, waiting for the bell. I couldn't stop myself. I had my hand up and was at the board and had it all solved in about ten seconds. The lads wanted to clap but they were afraid. After that Finch never asked me a question again and used to send me around the whole school collecting for the black babies when he was doing the sums class. I used to do nearly everyone's ecker on the way into school and even Bantam let me join his gang. And when I got first in the class that Christmas no one slagged me when I went up to get my prize. There was a hamper and a bottle of whiskey and a picture of Jesus and a crib. I'd promised Da I'd bring home the whiskey but the picture of Jesus was sort of magic and I hoped he wouldn't mind. It was the first time I'd ever seen Jesus with a smile on his face. His beard was very short. It was exactly what I wanted to look like when I was older. I brought it home in my schoolbag and brought it up to my room. I took it out of the glass frame very carefully and stared at it for a long time – just looking at His eyes. I knew I'd never let Him down and would always keep my promise to believe in miracles, and get everyone else to believe in them as well. That convinced Ma I was going to be a priest and she had loads of them calling in for a few weeks and Bobby had a lonely time stuck in the backyard. She pretended they were here to see Uncle Mick who was laid up with arthritis in the back bedroom. I knew they were there to tell me about my vocation but it frightened the life out of Uncle Mick and he was back on his feet in no time, even before I could give him a cure.

I liked the Franciscans the best. Their leader used to love animals, especially dogs, and they all wore beards and had a brilliant place out in Gormanstown that they brought me to once. Two football fields and a handball alley and right beside the beach. But I saw one of them in the distance whack a horse with a stick so I didn't bother with them after that. And anyway I'd a bigger job to do and I wasn't going to forget that.

Padraig Downey had got only a few stitches in his knee after the Croke Park accident and didn't even have to go to hospital, but his ma got a solicitor to sue them for loads of money. They wanted us to do the same and said we could share the costs and we'd get a right few bob out of them, and anyway, I wasn't the same child after what happened and would probably need treatment later in life and that could be very expensive. But Ma said that would be a very unlucky thing to do, and there wasn't a scrap wrong and if there was ever a problem our family were quite capable of looking after our own affairs and sent her about her business. I don't think Ma liked her very much, especially after Mrs Downey told the whole neighbourhood about her daughter's knickers being pulled down. Then Ma had a great idea. She got me to write in to the man in charge of Croke Park and tell him about my accident, about how I was afraid to stand in a big crowd at the matches any more, which was true. He wrote me back a lovely letter that allowed me get free tickets for the sideline for the next three years and I could bring a friend. Even though I fought with him nearly all the time, Shea was really my best friend and we went to all the matches together.

The sideline seats were great, especially for the hurling matches when the men would break their hurleys over another man's back, and throw the two bits towards us. Nobody would ever give out to you for picking up the two pieces and sticking them back together with metal bands that Da could do in his garage, and we'd always have enough fixed hurleys for nearly two teams. But my pals on the street liked playing soccer better so it was very hard to get them out to Fairview Park to play a real hurley match, and Da said if we didn't use them he wouldn't fix them any more and he'd throw them all out because there wasn't enough room in the back kitchen to even park his bike – they were taking up so much space. And that night when we went for our walk he told me for the first time about our great grandfather, Art O'Neill, who played in goal for Tipperary in 1916 and won an All Ireland Medal in 1921 as well. He used to smoke a cigarette when the play was at the other end, leaning on the goalpost, and was the first and only goalie ever to score a point from a puck out in Jones's Road which was the same place as

Croke Park before it changed its name. That's when I decided to become a goalie for Dublin and got Shea and Kevin O'Farrell and Padraig Downey, who'd got the stitches out of his knees now, to practise taking penalties against me on the pitch in Fairview Park and even Bobby my dog left the ball alone because he knew I was deadly serious. It might sound silly but I knew which side they'd shoot at. They hardly ever scored a goal – especially with the real *sliothar* – even when it was wet. Maybe a few points high in the air but I swear to God I could throw my hurley up high and even save some of them.

My other best pal Sean Kelly, who I'd split over the head a year ago with my hurley, had joined St Lawrence O'Toole's GAA club. I think it must have been for the Irish dancing because he had a lame leg from the TB and could never play a real match, but he was very fond of the girls, and hardly any boys went to the dances so he had most of the girls to himself. But he must have told some of the men from the club that I was a great goalie, because they called down to our house one day to sign me up.

I'd never played a real match before so I was very nervous, but decided to give it a go. They had a big house in Seville Place and their own pipe band with drummers and everything. They used to march in the Corpus Christi procession in June when all the coloured flags and bunting would be put up and altars to the Sacred Heart outside all the flats in Sheriff Street. I was an altar boy then and it was the only time Clicky Kelly's gang couldn't attack you. St Lawrence O'Toole's had won the best pipe band in Ireland and they marched out to Fairview Park in front of all the hurlers because it was such a big final. Even Ma and Da came out even though I was only a sub, because their real goalie was from O'Connell's school and was very famous. That was OK by me because if we won I'd still get a silver medal with a Celtic cross and even Tommy had never won one of those.

Even before the match started the two O'Meara brothers with red hair who played fullback were beating the lard out of their forwards. The team from Artane were tough enough and there was a huge row before the referee got a chance to blow the whistle for the start and our goalie got a belt of a hurley and lost all his teeth. He wanted to play on but his ma came over and told them what they could do with their hurling final and dragged him away.

I was so nervous I had to go to the toilet in the smelly shed before I could take his place, but it was a lovely big jersey all in green down past my knees and I felt very proud. When the match started and all the play was at the other end I just kept hitting my legs with the hurley to stop them shaking. The O'Meara brothers were brilliant and I didn't even have to save one shot, except when they got a penalty because Kevin O'Meara had hit his marker across the nose and made him bleed. We were winning by a mile anyway so I was ready. It all seemed in slow motion. I just looked at his eyes as he hit it and dived to my left and caught the ball. They were all on top of me in seconds, pulling and swiping and cursing, but I never let go of the ball. Then the O'Mearas came in and let fly with their hurley sticks. I could hear the screams and howls all around me but I kept my head down in the muck and never opened my eyes. Everyone was so busy hitting each other that when I had a peep with one eye I could see the whole pitch empty in front of me, so I snook out between their legs and solo'd the ball like I used to do in Emerald Street running to meet Da. I took a shot towards the empty goal. It went wide, but it didn't matter. I was a hero, but how could I tell them I was afraid to play for them again?

There was a great party in the club that night. Sean Kelly, my friend who'd got me into all this trouble, was dancing with every girl in sight. I sat in a corner drinking tea with Marietta biscuits. I was staring at my medal and didn't know how to tell them I was giving the whole thing up. I needn't have worried. Ma sorted the whole thing out. She told the man from the club the next morning when she met him in our butcher's that I had had a serious head condition and wasn't allowed play any more. I pretended to be really angry for two weeks and went into a sulk, but not too much because I didn't want her to change her mind. The men in the club were very kind to me and said I could be a drummer in the band if I liked. I didn't do that, but they had my name in the paper for saving a goal and I was the only one on our street that ever had their name in the paper twice in the one year. The next year I had my name in the paper again but only once, for winning a prize in a painting competition, when I had to go back into hospital for my head thing. But that was ages away, and how could I know about it then?

You'd never walk to Dollymount, always run, turn left at Darcy's shop on the corner. It wasn't really Darcy's any more. Old man Darcy had died and Ma said he was the last real gentleman on the street. He'd write the messages in a book and you didn't have to pay until you had the money, although my ma never did that, and right beside the shop Mad Micky Tohill lived. Like me he had something wrong with his head, but his wound was different. It was from the war, and he was definitely a bit mad or simple. Father Williams when he was alive would give out hell to him the way he would shout out the wrong words for the hymns at benediction and he'd always walk down the aisle of the church at funerals with his hand on the coffin, and everyone, especially the strangers, would think he was best pals with the corpse and give him a few bob.

One day he had a terrible row with me. He used to deliver the milk from Darcy's shop to most of the houses on our street. That same day my ma had forgotten her gloves at mass and when she went back to the church they were gone. When I opened the door to Mad Micky Tohill that morning to collect the milk he was wearing my ma's gloves, and when I shouted in to tell Ma he gave me a box on the face and said I was a cheeky young pup and that he'd never walk any of our coffins down the aisle. My ma had to give him a shilling to calm him down and pretend to give out to me. That was the day I realised he wasn't mad at all, and I decided to keep an eye on him.

The next man to buy Darcy's shop was young and very tall, and all the mas used to say he'd be a great catch. He'd even let you play a football match in his shop with a tennis ball when things were quiet and use old biscuit tins for the goals. Once when he was playing with us on the street Granny Wilson called the police and we were all arrested and had to give our names. James Connolly and Kevin Barry got into big trouble because the police wouldn't believe them, but only the nice man from Darcy's shop had to go to court and he got the Probation Act.

Once you turned the corner into Seville Place you'd have to put your dog on a lead 'cos there was loads of traffic up and down to the docks all day. Sometimes the men driving the horse and carts would let you have a ride, but hardly ever on a Thursday because that's when they got paid and they were like a chariot race to get to the pub. Once I had Bobby it was very hard not to step on the lines on the path; he'd be pulling so hard so I used to run fast, taking big steps. Three hundred and twenty-three was my best record, but that was the day Clicky Kelly and his gang from the flats were chasing us, and they caught Kevin O'Farrell and broke his glasses. They were the toughest gang of the whole lot and we made a big mistake. The next day old Mrs Lacey from next door asked us to go up to Ball Alley pub and get her a baby Powers. It was just me and Kevin and we had stuck his glasses together with some tape. We were in the pub giving out hell about Clicky Kelly. We didn't realise his mother was listening in the snug and it was all-out war after that. Thank God I had Bobby.

Once you reached the top of Seville Place you turned right at the Five Lamps, down onto North Strand, where the German bombers during the war blew up loads of people, all because we'd sent fire brigades up to Belfast to put out the huge fires. Da told me all about it. I used to play with his fire helmet and gas mask that he kept under the stairs. He was in the civil defence then and was the chief fire-engine driver of the whole lot. I loved that story and the one about him keeping the pigeons, but when he'd tell me about when he was only seven and saw the Black and Tans killing his two older cousins, I'd nearly go mad and it'd put you off the English for life and I couldn't blame him for being a Republican. Uncle Mick had a picture of Michael Collins in the hall, and nearly every Friday night when I'd be waiting for Da to come in after his Guinness (I'd know his knock on the letter box), I'd make sure to let him in quietly and help him hang his coat on the hanger in the hall, and he'd nearly always stick his tongue out at the picture and wink at me and give me my wages. Halfway down the North Strand I'd try and get Bobby to slow down outside the Strand Picture House to see what was on. It was sixpence in, but mostly my pocket money from Da wouldn't last till Sunday but that didn't matter.

Uncle Mick had loads of money. His job was to drive the cattle all the way down from the North Circular Road where the farmers would leave them and hunt them onto the Liverpool ship. He had a big stick with a nail at the end and sometimes he'd let you have a go, but never when they were hunting a bull. Once, Mad Micky Tohill thought he'd try it and came out with his own stick and the bull escaped and there was a huge row. It was right down on the docks, and the bull had got stuck in the passenger corridor. The ship was delayed for five hours and after that Uncle Mick never gave Micky the time of day. But on the Sunday, if me and Shea were broke, I wouldn't hypnotise Uncle Mick any more, so we'd just shout to him, 'We're off now, Uncle.' He was a bit deaf and you might have to shout it a few times, but in the end he'd always slip you a tanner as he settled in to listen to the match on the radio. He'd write the scores down on the back of a cornflakes box with a pencil – goals, points, frees, everything, and the only thing you'd have to do when you came home was add them all up because he never believed the commentators, especially when Wexford were playing.

When you were leaving the pictures on Sunday you'd have to be very fast off the mark 'cos the crowd in the fourpenny rush would chase you home to rob any money you'd left, especially if you'd been sitting in the balcony.

Bobby always knew when we were near Fairview Park. He'd be coughing and choking with excitement until you crossed East Wall Road and could let him off. First thing I ever remember in the pram is Fairview Park, and the woman leaning in to give me a red lollipop. I must have been at least two 'cos Aunt Bridie was pushing the pram and wouldn't let me suck it in case I choked. That must have been when a bird robbed the lollipop. I asked her afterwards and she thought it was a seagull and she said Ma was in the hospital getting my younger brother Shea at the time and my cousin Damian was with me in the pram but I don't remember that. Damian was my favourite cousin and when their da had TB they came to stay with us but where they all fitted I don't know.

Uncle Mick was minding the cattle every night on the Liverpool ship and they must have stayed in his big dark room with no electricity yet and you'd be afraid to go near it at night-time. I was about seven then and Damian used to be in my class. Our teacher Mrs Farrell was a bigger Republican than Da and would teach us that song that always made her cry – 'Wrap the green flag around me boys' – and she used to be in Cumann na mBan, the Irish girl soldiers' army, years ago when she was young. She wasn't too cross with you over sums, but she'd go mad if you didn't know your Irish. One day she asked Damian to spell '*uisce*'. He didn't know and he was sitting in the desk right in front of me and I didn't want him to get into trouble so I started writing the letters on his back very slowly with my finger, but she caught me and beat the living daylights out of me with a stick. That was the day I split Sean P. Kelly's head with my hurley because he was jeering Damian about being stupid. When his ma came around to complain I got thumped all over again and it was an awful long time before I had my next fight.

Bobby, my dog, would get fed up with me if I stopped in Fairview Park and asked the lads playing twenty-a-side football for any chance of a game and he'd just roam off on his own. After about two hours he'd come back and start barking at everyone and chasing the ball. One time he caught it and burst it and I had to pretend I didn't own him. They were chasing and cursing at him and I had to pretend to do that too. It took a long time for them all to leave and then I sat beside him on the hill in the park and had to pet him for ages before he'd go on the lead. But on the days going out to Dollymount I'd never stop in the park. We'd run straight through past the red bandstand and out to Clontarf. If the tide was out, he'd go over the rocks and straight down on the sand. He'd run nearly a mile out chasing birds, but hated getting wet and when the sea was full in and bashing off the rocks, he'd slink by my feet and bark like a wolf and stay on the grass.

Brother Finch was the curse of my life. No matter what you did on Sunday, you couldn't enjoy it because you knew you had to face the evil eye on Monday morning. Since the head accident he didn't really bother me that much, but I hated the way he bullied everyone else. One of my pals, Luke Nelson, used to get sick every Monday morning in the lane on the way to school, and no matter how many times I told him that we'd only a few weeks left with the bastard, and that we'd be moving up to Brother Judge's class who was very fair, he'd still vomit the minute he'd turn the corner and see the school gates.

Brother Judge was the only good thing about Mondays. He'd started up a harmonica band at half four every Monday after school. You had to put in sixpence every week to buy the harmonica, but even if you couldn't pay it he'd still buy it for you so long as you turned up for practice. I'd heard he never gave anyone a belt no matter what, so nobody ever let him down. There was forty-three of us in the band, and when he thought we were good enough he got the priests to buy us all green jackets and long white trousers and we played our first concert in St Francis Xavier Hall. We started with three marches, 'The Rising of the Moon' and two others. Then some waltzes, the Vienna one I think, and three of us were allowed play a solo of Elvis Presley's 'Wooden Heart'. Luke Nelson couldn't really play but Brother Judge let him stand up there in his band uniform and mime it, and two other boys who joined late were allowed play the triangle.

We only had one but they took it in turns and they put our picture in the *Irish Press* two weeks later.

Poxy Finch went mad the night after the concert because none of us had our ecker done. That was the day we heard him and Brother Judge having a row in the corridor about playing foreign music and that was the day I really knew that if I kept the deal I'd made with God in Croke Park, I really could do anything.

Brother Finch came back into the class in a fouler with a big red face and his forehead sweating. He had his leather out and called Luke Nelson's name out to say the Irish poetry about Raftery that we were supposed to learn, but didn't have time to. All the fun of last night drained from Luke Nelson's face. He was nearly going to faint – so I asked God to save him, and really believed it would happen even as poxy Finch went towards him with the leather. I didn't know what was going to happen but I knew for absolute certain that something would. Next minute Luke blurted out in English, 'I'm Raftery the poet, full of hope and love/Having eyes without sight, lonely I rove. *Is Mise Raifterí an file, lán dóchais is grádh/Le súilibh gan solus, le ciúnas gan crádh.*'

Finch nearly had a heart attack. He almost fell back between the desks. He muttered something about needing to learn the rest of it, but we could all see he was stunned and Luke Nelson's face was bright, shining in the sun through the classroom window. Then Brother Judge came in and said he needed all his harmonica boys urgently to practise for a new concert in the Theatre Royal in Hawkins Street, that it would be a great honour for the school, and we'd be playing with Tommy Dando and his Lowry Organ the next Saturday night, and we had to learn a few new songs. Then Brother Frampton, the head of all the Christian Brothers in our school, came in and said the band was a credit to the parish and told Finch not to give us any ecker for the week. That's when I got my first big headache, and it always happened after that when the magic happened, but not as bad as that first time. I went home and went straight to bed with the pain. I told Ma I had a toothache because I didn't want to tell her the truth or she might send me back into hospital, so I took out my picture of Jesus and put it under my pillow and the pain went away.

Luke Nelson died even before Uncle Mick and before Finch could get back at him. It was May and it had been really sunny for weeks. They were swimming in Spencer Docks when a young boy got into trouble and was going down for the third time. I wasn't there because we weren't allowed, but they told me afterwards that Luke just jumped straight in in his clothes to save him and never came back up. It was the first death in our parish that I could remember of anybody young. All the hurlers from St Lawrence O'Toole's, that I used to play for, criss-crossed their hurleys over the coffin as a mark of respect. Even the O'Meara brothers and everyone was crying. And Mad Micky Tohill, who didn't know what was happening, walked down the aisle with his hand on the white coffin and tears in his eyes. I tried not to cry because I was doing altar boy with the thurible and you're not supposed to. Then Tommy Bantam shoved his way through the crowd and put the picture of the harmonica band on the coffin and you could see Luke's smiling face, and none of us, not even poxy Finch, could hold back the tears. The next week was the saddest ever in our class. There was an article in one of the papers, very small, under the end of a column about farm prices in Mayo. We all cut it out and kept it.

'Luke Nelson – a young Dublin hero.'

Brother Finch never mentioned his name once, although his desk was empty and his books were still there. But Father McOrly came into the class one Friday before the school holidays and gave a talk about Luke and about heroes and about the love of Jesus for all children. Then he took the whole class up to the Savoy cinema to see *Robin Hood* and brought us all into the Savoy Grill for tea, and Da said afterwards that if you looked hard enough there were still a few saints wearing white collars but they were few and far between.

Aunt Chrissie and Uncle Andy had bought a huge new house in Coolock. He wasn't my real uncle because they weren't married yet, but she was allowed stay in the new house so long as they each had their own room. Ma said a lot of our neighbours were very narrow-minded and should mind their own business, but when any of them asked Ma she'd say Chrissie was doing extra night duty up in the hospital, saving for her big day. I was let go stay with them sometimes on my own. You had to tell the man on the 42 bus to let you off at the house with the television aerial, even though it wasn't plugged in yet.

They had a massive garden at the back. Uncle Andy had it all dug up in rows for potatoes and cabbage and stuff and he'd let you help if you'd brought your wellies. There was a grass patch at the end and he'd let you practise taking penalties on him with a real leather football because he played for Buccaneers. He said I had green fingers and wasn't it a pity I didn't have a small piece of garden for myself. That's when I got the idea of asking our next-door neighbours the Reddings about practising with the rhubarb. They had a proper garden with grass and they let me use the back of it. That worked so well and so quick that Ma was able to make rhubarb tart nearly every day until the whole family was getting diarrhoea and she had to stop.

Uncle Andy was allowed practise tickling Chrissie in bed at night-time and he'd get me to help. She'd laugh so much she'd scream at us to stop and one night the next-door neighbour rang the bell and told Andy to keep the noise down, and he was a disgrace because they weren't even married yet. The only thing I hated there was Chrissie would always make you say the rosary with loads of extra bits, but at least it was always the joyful or the glorious mysteries.

At home during Lent Ma would always say the sorrowful ones and I often wondered about that. Ma and Chrissie and Bridie would do novenas together for special petitions. But they hardly ever worked. They always put in a safeguard for God so they couldn't blame Him when it failed – 'if it be Thy will'. I knew all you had to do was really believe and it always worked. I'd promised God that day in Croke Park that I'd tell everyone, but I wasn't ready yet because I needed to keep practising. But one night when I was staying with Chrissie, and we'd locked Andy out of the bedroom because he was messing too much, I heard her coming to the end of her prayers and saying, 'Dear God, if it be Your will, please get the television man to call and fix up the aerial.' I loved Chrissie so decided to give her a hand. I told her to ask for a bigger petition, but she said no, God was busy with famines and everything, and she felt bad even praying for that. When she was asleep, I just put my hand on my picture of Jesus, and couldn't wait to answer the door to the television man the next day, because I'd asked God to make sure he came early before Chrissie went to work. I didn't know why she even bothered praying for that because the next night, when me and Andy sat watching football, she spent about three hours in her room giving thanks, and never watched a thing.

My ma's other sister, Bridie, and her family, who'd all come to stay with us when Uncle Phil had TB, had just got a new house up in Marino. I loved going to stay there as well. She was a great cook and hardly ever made rhubarb tarts. Ma thought my cousins were a bit wild and always warned me not to get into trouble up there, but they weren't really, only Dermot who used to practise being Superman from his bedroom window, but he broke his two legs on the day of his communion and tore his new trousers. Adrian was the youngest and much quieter than the others, but he was a great poet and was learning the drums. I told him he could join our harmonica band when me and Mary Joe set it up, so one day he carried all his drums down to Emerald Street to practise with us, but he could hardly talk when he came in and whispered he was too bollixed to lift a snare. All my cousins were great cursers but luckily no one heard him and Da gave him a sneaky swig out of his Guinness and told him he'd be gameball.

They had a car of their own and nearly always drove down to Dollymount on summer Sundays. Da loved it when they'd all come. You could stand on a hill and watch out for them driving across the wooden bridge in the distance. Da and Uncle Phil would sit in the hollow with hankies on their heads waiting for the kettle to boil. Ma and Bridie would spread out all the sandwiches on a blanket and we'd all climb into the golf course and race after Bobby when he'd be chasing the hares. Uncle Mick never came with us to Dollymount but, like us, our cousins had an Aunt Gen staying with them in their house. She'd always come and bring hundreds of scones and butter. She was really skinny and at least as old as Uncle Mick, but when we were all playing hide-and-seek she was terrible hard to catch, and if you did you'd be afraid you might break her ribs. You'd be tired and sunburnt on the way home, but the happiest ever because there were never any rows.

There was a photograph of Ma and Da on the piano in the parlour. I used to practise on it every Sunday morning after ten mass until the corned beef was ready at one o'clock. I didn't like vegetables but Ma would let me eat raw cabbage and turnips because I hated the smell of them when they were cooked. The photograph was in black and white but I remembered Da told me once his suit was really brown. Ma had a big black hat with a feather in it and they went to Limerick on their honeymoon. Ma and Da looked a bit nervous in the photograph but they were very young and at least they were holding hands. The piano had a few notes missing but you could still play a tune if you stuck to the right-hand side. So could Da but at least he was able to use his two hands and I often wondered who had taught him that. Ma sent Elaine to learn the piano. She hated it and never practised but later when she met Joe Connolly that was going to marry her, she spent hours locked in the parlour practising the guitar with him because they were going to start up a band, and they'd never let you go in and listen to them playing.

Ma and Da looked very young in the photograph and when I'd take a break in my Sunday morning practising, I'd often wonder how they saved up enough money for such lovely clothes. I know Da had a great job in a garage in Clontarf – the one Ma was always giving out to him about not buying, and I don't think he drank much then so he would have been able to save a bit, but I don't think Ma earned that much as a secretary even though her boss Mr Smith said she was the best he'd ever seen. Maybe Uncle Mick lent them a few bob, but I know they got a big flat in Clontarf and that's where I was born in the nursing home there. Ma said three weeks too early because a bee stung her on the leg and that must have brought me on. Her neighbour stopped a bus and told the driver to turn off the road and rush her straight to the nursing home. I was born with a caul that Ma took home with her and stuck on tracing paper. She kept it in the tin box with our old photographs and you had to be very careful taking it out to look at it because it was nearly eleven years old. Everyone said it was very lucky to be born with a caul and the sailors would pay a lot of money for it because it meant you'd never drown.

One day in Dollymount I decided to see if it was really true. I went out very deep near Curley's Hole where kids drowned every year. I tried to go down three times but the water was freezing like ice. I couldn't bear it and decided to wait for a warmer day. Anyway my cousins were roaring from the shore that our picnic was ready and my lips were blue. Maybe the caul saved me in Croke Park on Patrick's Day, but I had a lot to do and never tried drowning again.

Every time I did a miracle I'd get a terrible headache, not like the one you get from eating ice cream too fast, but much worse and it lasted a long time. When it got too bad I'd go to bed and pull the blanket over my head until it went away. I always told Ma it was a toothache because it wasn't time to tell her yet. Poor Mr Reddy our dentist was worn out checking my teeth and finding nothing wrong. He said it must be neuralgia or bad circulation and told Ma I should get out a bit more and not be reading too much. I had to give up soccer because the doctor that nearly operated on me said it would be too dangerous to heady the ball. Ma didn't want me hurling any more so I took up running and I loved that. You had to start slow because if you didn't you'd have to stop after ten minutes to get your breath. You'd get a terrible pain in your appendix and that was very dangerous for you if it turned out to be acute. Once you got your second wind it was brilliant, you wouldn't know how far you'd gone or even where you were. You could just go inside your head. You'd forget all your troubles and just feel the sweat on your forehead and the wind on your face. You could hear the birds chirping in the park above the noise of the traffic and have any dream you wanted. My favourite one was scoring the winning goal for Dublin in Croke Park with my head and I'd forget I wasn't allowed do that. No one had broken the four-minute mile, and when I'd get to Clontarf I'd go as fast as I could and count up to two hundred and forty seconds, but I could never remember which lamp-post I'd start and finish at. I was going to get Da to measure it when he had a car to test drive, but really I couldn't care and I'd just keep running. In my dream I'd always end up back in Croke Park, and this time I'd be in goal saving a penalty.

One day I was running four steps for every breath and looking at the footpath in front of me. It was evening and quiet and I forgot even to count the lamp-posts as they flew by. I knew I was going uphill and I didn't want to look up. Everything went quiet around me – no traffic, no lights, no birds, just the sound and feel of my feet on the path and the rhythm of my breath. One two three four in, one two three four out. It was like floating in space.

When I looked up everything looked different, everything had changed. I was on the top of Howth Hill. The sea stretched for miles and was the deepest blue I'd ever seen. The green grass and the purple heather were gently swaying in the breeze and behind me high up on the hill was a big white house shining in the sun, looking right across the bay. I sat down in the calmness and didn't even have to catch my breath. There was no one around anywhere and the grass was so high. I took off all my clothes and lay back in the sun. I could feel the grass tickling my bum and my shoulder and my skin felt so alive all over. It was the happiest I had ever been. I closed my eyes and was smiling because I remembered the picture on the piano, of Ma and Da holding hands. If I opened my eyes and leaned my head backwards I could see the big white house and I thought I'd love to live there. I wondered when would I get married and who would she be. Would she be as beautiful as Ma in that picture? I lay on my tummy and started picking buttercups – she loves me, she loves me not, she loves me. A little cloud came across the sun and I remembered I hadn't done a miracle for a long time and it wasn't the headaches. I knew once I started my job I could never be the same. Never this free. Then the sun came back out and I remembered Jesus did loads of them but never told anyone about his job until he was thirty, so I could have more time. It was the greatest feeling in the world. I rolled down the hill laughing and shouting and only stopped when I bumped into a furze bush. Then I heard some people chatting in the distance and I quickly put my clothes back on. It was a long way home and my legs were sore but it was down-hill all the way and it was a perfect day.

Mr Reddy our dentist had a big house too, on Westland Row, but it wasn't white. His wife or his girlfriend was very young and she'd always hold your hand and squeeze it when he'd stick the needle into your gum and he had a puppet monkey that he'd do the ventriloquist with to take your mind off the pain. The worst day was when I got my front tooth knocked out in street hurling. He told Ma I was too young for a false one but he had a great idea. If I stuck pared down matchsticks between all my teeth at night-time when I was going to bed, it wouldn't take too long to move them all around and fill the gap. You'd be lying in bed with all these bits of timber sticking out of your mouth. It was very hard to talk and I couldn't frighten Shea any more with my ghost stories, but at least you had a chance to think, and to listen to all the neighbours going home from the pub.

When I was brought back to see Mr Reddy over the headaches that I pretended were toothaches, he was delighted and said the gap was so small now I'd hardly be able to whistle Dixie through it. At least he'd got me into the running, but he must have said something to Ma that I didn't hear, because it wasn't long before she dragged me off to an eye doctor, even though the headaches had nearly stopped. The eye man must have been very famous because we had to wait three and a half weeks for an appointment and you had to pay in advance. I heard Da say in the kitchen one night when I was listening outside the door that if things went on like this he'd have to get a second job, and he told Ma to stop fussing like this, that there was nothing wrong with the child, so I was determined not to let him down, and pass the eye test at first go.

He was a baldy man, but he had glasses himself so I thought he couldn't be great at his job. When I was standing in the room and he was taking down my details from Ma, I saw the chart on the wall with all the letters and numbers. I learned them all off by heart real quick. I had to move a bit closer to see the tiny ones at the bottom, but they never noticed. Then when he put me sitting in the chair, left eye, right eye, I never made a mistake and he was a bit surprised. He told Ma everyone had a lazy eye and this was a bit strange. He got this little torch thing and started staring into my eyes. There was a smell off his breath but I was hoping he wouldn't see anything wrong and catch me out. He was humming and hawing for a while and saying, 'Mmmm'. Then he went back to the chart and turned it over and I had to start again. I made a total bollix of it. Then he kept going, 'Aha – aha!' and went back to the first chart. I'd got so frightened I'd forgotten what was on it and suddenly I was in big trouble . . . He took Ma aside and had a quiet whisper with her and wrote out something on his writing pad to give her.

'There you are, young Mr O'Neill, you're a smart young man, but I think you have a slight problem.' He was really angry. I could see by the red on his face, and as I followed Ma out the door, he deliberately stood hard on my toe. Ma never said a word to me all the way home but I knew by the look on her face she wanted to give me a good box on the ear, but maybe she was afraid because of my head thing, or maybe she felt sorry for me because he'd told her there was something seriously wrong.

My ma's best pal Theresa used to come down to visit her every Monday night. They used to work together in Evans Medical Supplies on the North Wall when Ma was a young girl. She was secretary to the boss and could do shorthand and typing, about six hundred words a minute I think, and Theresa was the phone secretary down there. They went everywhere together, to plays and dances and even to Blackpool once on an office trip where everyone else but them got drunk and made a show of themselves. And they both got husbands out of it 'cos Da used to fix up all the vans for their delivery men and even then he was the best motor mechanic in Ireland. I don't know how Theresa met her husband, Tom Moynihan, but his father was very rich and used to sign every single pound note in Ireland that was ever printed, even though he was only a secretary but it was for the Department of Finance.

Ma would always tell Theresa her secrets and if there was no one else in the kitchen and you went out the back to make them a cup of tea you could sneak back and hear everything outside the door. That's how I heard for the first time about Da's pain in his stomach, and how he wasn't eating much and vomiting, and sneaking half his dinner down under the table to Bobby, but I knew she was wrong about that, because it was only ever headaches with him, and I could always fix them. But that same night I heard her telling Theresa that she was very worried about me and that there was definitely something wrong with my head. Then she went into a whisper and no matter how hard I pushed my ear against the keyhole, I couldn't hear a thing, only at the very end that the eye man had given her a referral for a private specialist in Fitzwilliam Square to examine my head and Theresa said do it sooner rather than later, Molly, but God was good, and maybe their novenas about my da's drinking would work.

But the novenas didn't work. The next Friday night Ma kept looking at the clock and when I'd finished my ecker about ten past nine, she asked me to call up to Noctor's pub and tell Da his grub was ready. She must have been terrible worried about him 'cos she'd never asked any of us to do that ever before.

I stood outside Noctor's hoping some of my da's pals would come out and I could get them to give Da the message. But I couldn't remember if he had any, or what they looked like, only Barney his foreman and I think he drank his Guinness somewhere else and it was freezing so I just went in. The place was fairly busy and very smoky but Da was sitting at the counter on his own. The pub man had just given Da a pint and I heard Da asking him to 'Throw us a chaser with that, Michael, like a good man.' I whispered 'Da' and when he looked around he looked surprised, but he wasn't cross with me.

'Michael, allow me to introduce one of my sons, and give him a glass of lemonade.' I whispered the message to Da, and he said everything would be as right as the mail and we'd go after I finished the lemonade. He put me sitting in the snug with two really old women. They must have been drinking chasers because the drinks looked the very same as the one Da had beside his Guinness. They were very nice to me and said my da was a lovely man and very generous to everyone when he got the bonus. On our way out the pub man called me over and gave me a shilling for myself. He was watching Da standing at the door talking to some man, so he leaned across the counter and said, very quietly, 'There's not many like your father. Keep an eye on him, son, make sure he looks after himself.' But I knew it was only the headaches.

On the way home I asked Da what a bonus was. He stopped and leaned against the Browns' railings, and made me promise I'd never mention the word 'bonus' in our house, especially to Ma. I meant to look it up in Aunt Chrissie's medical book anyway, just in case it was a rare deadly incurable disease or something, but I never did.

My friend Sean Kelly got a girlfriend from the hurling club. Her name was Marie O'Reilly. He let me dance with her once but she always smelt very sweaty. She had a great da called Mr O'Reilly with a big moustache who'd let you call him Liam. He was a bus conductor on the 24 bus from Marino that would bring you into town. Every week on Saturday morning, I had to go over to Merrion Square for the new specialist Ma had got me, to do these head-test exams. Ma would give me the bus fare, but once you knew what time his bus would drive by at he'd never charge you and you could spend your fare buying toy soldiers in Woolworths on Grafton Street, or have a chocolate cake in the Swiss Chalet restaurant on Stephen's Green. I got fed up with the head tests; they were always the same. Match up dots and pictures, colour in squares and rectangles, and learn off and remember ten words in a row. Just to annoy him I'd make a balls of the last one because I don't think he ever looked up the results. But I loved walking up Grafton Street with the smell of coffee from Bewley's. We only ever got Irel coffee and it never smelt the same. I never did it but you could go into Bewley's and order a plate of cream cakes. They'd leave six in front of you, but even if you ate them all you could get away with just paying for one. I was afraid to steal so I never did it. But I did do a robbery once in Woolworths.

I was collecting a whole set of tin soldiers from Woolworths, one a week. It was the US cavalry and a big bunch of Indians. Their chief Cochise was the last one I needed but he was threepence dearer than the others so I left him till last. One Saturday morning I was looking at him for about ten minutes. His clothes were bright yellow and he had red, green and white feathers. He cost ninepence and I didn't have enough money, even if I walked home. A boy with glasses picked him up and asked the man behind the counter how much he cost. The man told him and that that was the last one left and they wouldn't be getting any more in. The boy ran off wiping his nose looking for his ma. I had to do it quick – I ran out of the shop with Cochise in my pocket and swore to myself that I'd pay them back next week.

Everything went bad for me that week. Da had a terrible pain in his stomach that I couldn't fix. Bobby bit Mrs Wilson because she made a kick at him and her ankle swelled up. She had to get the doctor and Ma had to pay for it. Then a letter came into the house about me not turning up for all the head tests.

I told my best friend Kevin O'Farrell about the problem. They had loads of money and he lent me the extra threepence. The next Saturday I was in Woolworths in Grafton Street the minute it opened. The man behind the counter couldn't understand a word I was saying I was stuttering so much, and wouldn't take the ninepence and told me to feck off and stop annoying him he had such a hangover. I threw Cochise back in the wrong place among a bunch of cowboys and ran out of the shop and didn't stop until I got to the clinic in the head place. Mr McIvor the head-doctor man gave me a good talking to about missing my classes. I was so relieved about not being caught out, I did all the tests brilliant and got a hundred out of a hundred and there was no letters home for a long time after that. But I still missed Cochise and they must have sold him because I never saw him in there again.

I felt so bad over the robbery that I decided to go for a big miracle. One of my friends, Peter Murray, whose family had moved from Ballyragget, had a brother called Joe that had incurable leukaemia and everyone on the street knew that meant he had only four months to live. He was an altar boy like me so he knew when he got extreme unction three times in one year that he was on the way out. He had lovely blond hair and was a year younger than me and all the girls were mad about him. But once he got sick, the blinds were always down in their house and you had to whisper when you called in to lend him comics. One night when I was sitting beside his bed reading him an adventure story about Irish warriors, because he loved Cuchulain, he fell asleep. There was sweat all over his face and I was afraid he'd die then and there. I put my hand on his forehead, but I didn't know if I was strong enough or good enough to try to fix him, and I didn't want to mess it up.

They were nearly the poorest family in the parish although his ma never went to the pawnshop. His da's coat was on top of the blanket on the bed but it couldn't stop him shivering in his sleep. He'd always wanted to go to Killarney because he said it was a magical place, and there was an old faded brown photograph in their hallway of the lakes and the waterfalls. They let me stay there one night when the doctor came in and I was holding his hand. I heard the doctor whisper that the best they could hope for was a remission that would give him an extra six months, so I decided that's what I'd go for, but when I was lying in bed that night I told God that he had to arrange a trip to Killarney for him before he died.

It didn't take long. About a week later, Father McOrly was in our house visiting Ma because they were great friends. He told Ma he was going on holidays for two weeks and would love to take me and Shea along for the first week. He was well got with the Christian Brothers and could get us off school. This was a huge thing. Ma was very proud and Da said it would be the making of us, and guess where he was taking us – to Kenmare in County Kerry. I looked it up on the map – only twenty miles from Killarney. I didn't wish it on him but Shea finally got the measles. Father McOrly was terrible disappointed and said it wouldn't be right to take me on my own. He'd done the three extreme unctions on Joe Murray, but I don't think even he realised how powerful God was. In about three days, Joe was up and about eating all his food and having rows with his ma when she was afraid to let him out to play. I was going to say something but I didn't have to. Father McOrly called in that week and said wouldn't it be a great idea and a blessing if he took me and Joe Murray with him and wouldn't it be a great thing for both of us. We were on our way.

We didn't have any cases or luggage bags or proper summer clothes but Father McOrly said he'd look after all of that and stopped at Frawley's in Thomas Street and bought us everything we needed. Then he called into

Alpha Bargains in Liffey Street and let us pick out Swiss army knives for hunting in the forests in Killarney and a whistle in case we got lost. My job was to look after Joe in case he got sick and we both had to do altar boys for Father McOrly at the seven o'clock mass every day in the nuns' convent in Kenmare where he was staying and would get his big breakfast. On the way down we stopped at this posh hotel in Limerick. Father McOrly loved his grub and we had a huge feed with loads of knives and forks. He showed us how you had to work from the outside in with the cutlery and always to drink your soup, though he said eat it, by pushing the soup spoon away from you and tilting the dish the other way. He said it was a very important thing to do it right, especially if we ever got married or were in business. He only had the one glass of wine and never even asked for a Guinness.

The road to Killarney was very twisty once you got near. It was a Volkswagen car with a funny smell off the dashboard when the sun was on it and I was the one to get sick. We stopped at Torc Waterfall and I couldn't believe it when Joe said he'd love to climb to the top. Father McOrly said he'd let us out and took out his box of snuff. Joe was up the steps on the side of the mountain like a goat and I couldn't keep up with him. When we reached the top, and before I could catch my breath, Joe was standing looking across the lakes and you never saw anything like the look on his face. It was exactly the same view in the old brown picture in the hall except this time it was in brilliant colours. He stood so long looking across at it that I was getting cold in my new short-sleeved shirt that Father McOrly bought for me. It was the strangest look ever – his eyes were the deepest blue. He started to say something then he stopped. I would have waited for ever up there with him. Then he gave me a shove and said, 'Race you to the bottom' and, of course, he won.

Our guest house in Kenmare wasn't that great. The people were very nice to us but a bit strange. Neither of us could understand a word they said and the food was terrible. They knew Joe wasn't well but everything they gave us to eat was lumpy. At least that's what I thought, but Joe would demolish the gristly meat and the sour buttermilk in seconds and I was always the one to get sick. He'd be up before me every morning shouting, 'Up – up – up – it's a lovely day!' and when the mass was over he'd have organised adventure and treasure hunts and swims until you'd be exhausted. The week went too fast and we thought Father McOrly would be sending us home on the train because he was going to visit his relations in Tramore in County Waterford for his last week. But he changed his mind that last day when we were in the shop buying souvenirs and postcards to bring home to our family. We were standing outside the shop and our clothes were already packed for the journey home. Joe Murray had bought loads of postcards of the Lakes of Killarney and he looked really sad. Father McOrly must have been a saint, because he pulled up in his car and said, 'C'mon lads – I'm taking ye with me to Tramore!'

I think Father McOrly was delighted he didn't have to stay with nuns in Tramore. All the way there he was singing and whistling. When we passed the sign saying 'Welcome to County Waterford' he stopped the car and we all got out.

'I'm home, boys, I'm home,' he said, because that's where he was from. He was a Republican like Da and didn't like Michael Collins very much so he was glad to have got through County Cork. We had a picnic in a field and he told us all about his youth. We were very polite and listened nicely but we were dying to get to Tramore with the long beaches and big sandhills and all the amusement arcades that he told us about. He was staying with a lovely family called the Walshes, whose da was a baker. They had their own altar boys in Tramore so we wouldn't have to serve mass and could spend the whole day wandering around by ourselves if we wanted to. When we got there it was nearly dark and the seafront was lit up by coloured flashing lights and carnival things. I knew Joe Murray was as excited as me, but we didn't want to show it in case Father McOrly thought we hadn't enjoyed Killarney.

Once he got us settled in our little hotel and he went off to meet the Walsh family, we started screaming and shouting and running around the room. I would have been happy enough to stay in that night but Joe Murray wasn't having any of it. He was sweating with excitement and maybe he didn't have long left anyway. So out we dashed straight down to the promenade. We spent the whole night and nearly all our money on the bumpers, crashing into girls. My voice hadn't broken yet and Joe Murray was very handsome with a man's voice because he'd already grown up. The girls were mad about him but I couldn't get a look in. At least he invited me along with the two girls he picked to go for a walk with him along the big beach. They were both linking him and I streeled along a bit behind skipping stones across the water and pretending I couldn't care less. Then he left me with the ugly one while he and his new girlfriend went into the sandhills for a kiss.

My one was called Marjorie, they were down from Donegal, and once you got used to the accent she wasn't really that bad. I showed her how to find a flat stone and throw it and make it skip on the water. We went in for a paddle. The sea was ice cold at the start. Then she came over and said would we have a go at kissing? It wasn't pitch dark so I could see she definitely wasn't that pretty. I told her I had chickenpox coming on, and it wouldn't be a good idea. Then the tide was coming in and our shoes and socks went floating by. We grabbed them and ran out and nothing could stop her roaring and crying so I gave her a hug. It wasn't bad and we decided to have a go at the kissing anyway. I don't think I was her first boyfriend because she had a funny way of sticking out her tongue and tickling your teeth. The moon had just broken free from the clouds. Luckily Joe Murray and his girlfriend came along because I hadn't a clue what to do next.

On the last day, like me, Joe Murray couldn't wait to get home. On the drive back, Father McOrly was a bit sad. We'd had loads of picnics with him in the sandhills and he'd let you roll him down the dunes. I often wondered what it would have been like if he'd got married and had kids of his own. But not to worry, God was good and had his own ways. Then he asked us to say a little prayer with him, but it was only one decade of the rosary and no trimmings, so that was OK. Then he turned to Joe Murray who was sitting in the passenger seat because it was his turn, and got Joe to promise him that, when he was an old man, Joe would take him for a drive down to Killarney when Joe was married with his own family. That was the best thing I ever heard a priest say to anyone and I think that's why Joe Murray didn't die.

Brother Finch was like a raging lunatic on that last day before the summer holidays. All the other classes were having great fun and we could hear them laughing and joking with their teachers, but Finch had us sweating over algebra for two hours and still handing out a few belts. I wondered what he'd do for his summer holidays. I couldn't imagine him in swimming trunks on a beach or going to football matches with his pals if he had any. I don't think any of the other Brothers liked him very much and I remembered that day after our concert when I heard

Brother Judge tell him in the corridor that he was a disgrace to the order, but as the clock ticked down towards four o'clock and freedom, I knew this was the last day he could ever torture us and we'd be moving up to Brother Judge's class next year, who'd let you act out the Irish history stories, and split the class in two for all the fights between the Irish and the English, and I hoped I'd be on Bantam's side, 'cos he was huge, even though the Irish never won because we always had a traitor on our side and God I hoped I wouldn't get that part.

I must have been looking out the window imagining the Battle of Kinsale and not paying attention when I got a belt on the face and was ordered to the blackboard to solve the equation. I got it right and that really annoyed him so he called up Bantam to do the next one and that was a fatal mistake. None of us knew that Bantam's da had told him he could give up school forever and go for a job on the docks. When Finch tried to give Bantam a few belts for not knowing the answer all hell broke loose. Bantam hit him straight in the face with the best punch I'd ever seen and Finch collapsed in a heap on the floor. Then Bantam told him what he could do with his fucking algebra and that he'd never be coming back again. We were all afraid to cheer in case Finch wasn't dead.

Then Paul Timmons, who'd got the hiding for calling him the Fucker Finch on the excursion, ran up the class and kicked him in the balls and said his da wouldn't let him come back to this kip either. We couldn't help it, after what had happened to Paul Timmons, and everyone cheered, especially when our hero Bantam rang the school bell and told us the class was over. Brother Judge tried to stop us at the door but we were all mad now and ran out into the yard screaming and shouting and went for a football match in Fairview Park. I'd taken one last look at Finch on the floor and his eye caught mine and I knew by the look of revenge on his face that I couldn't go back. I'd have to persuade Da to let me train to be a hypnotist or a carpenter, or maybe even help him fix cars, because I'd never be able to face Finch again. But I wouldn't tell him about the miracles yet.

Auntie Chrissie, my ma's youngest sister who used live in the house with us, was lovely and very kind and would never squeal your secrets on you, so that night I told her my plan about giving up school forever. She was always laughing, especially when she'd let you put the red varnish on her toenails. I loved the smell off the bottle and the way she'd go into hysterics if you tickled her feet. She thought it would be a better plan for me to say nothing to Ma and Da and enjoy my summer holidays and not decide on anything until the end of them, and she gave me half a crown towards my new bicycle that I was saving to buy at the police auction, because Da's was too big and heavy and anyway he nearly always used it except on Friday nights and Saturdays and Sundays, but I was still dying to tell him my plan.

It's easy to make a cricket bat. You just need a small plank of wood and a good saw. Then you chalked out the wicket on the convent gate and you'd always use a tennis ball because a *sliothar* was too hard and dangerous. Nobody could ever agree when you were bowled out so one day I found a tin of red paint in the shed in our yard and painted the ball. If there was a red mark on the wicket then you were definitely out, but all the bowlers had red hands and you'd forget and be sweating and wipe your forehead or rub your hands on your jumper, and we weren't allowed do that again.

The Reddings' house next door was right opposite the wicket, but they were very good and never gave out when the ball would smash off it, except the day I hit it straight through their fanlight. They were away on holidays in Loughshinney and it was a terrible start to the first day of my summer holidays.

They were two old spinsters and their bachelor brother who nearly got married once but was let down at the altar and never came out of his house again except to go to mass. They were very good to me after letting me grow all that rhubarb in their back garden, so I couldn't let them down.

Luckily there was no one in my house so we dragged out our big table to stand on and pulled out the broken glass. I'd seen Uncle Mick fixing one of our windows once so I knew exactly what to do. I cut out a piece of cardboard exactly in the shape of the fanlight, got my money for the police-auction bike and about eleven of us went up to Amiens Street to the glass shop. The man there was very nice and had the glass cut in no time. He even gave us loads of extra putty and just as well, it was about two inches short the whole way round. We did our best but there were still a few huge gaps, but at least it stayed in place. We gave up the cricket after that and no one noticed a thing, and to tell the truth we forgot about it ourselves because the marble season was starting. It was only later that winter, one day when I was in borrowing an Agatha Christie book off them, and the three of them were sitting around their fire with their coats on, reading and eating sweets and giving out about the terrible draught, that I remembered. They were right – it was freezing in their hall and all over the house, but it was too late to do anything about it, so I just prayed none of them would catch pneumonia, or if they did that I wouldn't be blamed.

But later that day Da cheered me up. I think he was beginning to believe that Ma was right, that maybe there really was something wrong with my head. I could tell by the way he'd look at me when he thought I wasn't noticing. So he'd borrowed an almost brand new Citroën belonging to the Archbishop. He collected me and brought me up to the garage where he worked and I was allowed sit in while he was fixing it. I knew he didn't like priests very much except Father McOrly, who brought all the altar boys out in turn to posh restaurants to teach them how to use the knives and forks from the outside in and spoon the soup away from you. Da was working away with his shiny spanner talking to Barney his foreman, and I was flicking the lights and beeping the horn, and searching inside the glove press. There was a bottle of whiskey in there. I knew Archbishops weren't allowed drink, so maybe it was a present for Da. Then I heard Da telling Barney that he'd spotted a bottle of whiskey in the glove compartment. Barney laughed and said, 'Sure it's all they have, celibacy is a tough call.' Da said, 'Tell me about it' and they both started laughing. I was glad Da had such a good pal especially when he let me play with the buttons on the lift for bringing the cars up and down.

It was only the second day of my school holidays and I'd spent most of my bike money on the Reddings' fanlight window that I broke playing cricket, but me and Shea went up to the police auction anyway. There was loads of stuff and hundreds of bikes with lot numbers on them. For a laugh we decided we'd pick out which bikes we would have bought. Shea found one with straight handlebars and three gears. I saw one all in red, even red mudguards. It had racing handlebars and no gears but I would have done anything to be able to buy it and when anyone else wandered over near it, I'd move straight in and pretend to be examining the wheels and shout across to Shea that the spokes and saddle were banjaxed on this heap of junk.

When the auction started it was amazing. There was a big crowd but you'd hardly notice who was bidding for anything, and when something was sold, they just came down and took your name. When it came close to the lot number for my bike my heart started thumping. I don't know what happened me; I must have gone mad or something. I started to put up my hand to bid for it. Shea was standing beside me whispering, 'Stop fuckin' messing, Robbie' but I couldn't help it. There was another man there up against me. He must have been loaded because he kept going up in five shillings. When it was three pounds ten a voice that must have been mine shouted out, 'Four pounds!' A few people looked around. So did I. Shea muttered, 'Aw Jaysus . . .' and squeezed towards the door. The man came down and gave me a docket and took my name. I had to give a wrong address and hoped Kevin O'Farrell wouldn't mind. I took a last look at my bike and sneaked out fast. Shea was waiting outside. He didn't give out to me and swore he wouldn't tell Ma. I think he felt sorry for me but we ran all the way home because there was an awful lot of guards around.

A few days later all our pals on the street were going on a bike excursion to Drogheda to see Oliver Plunkett's head. Shea got a loan of a girl's bike off Lily Downey. It was Saturday so I could take Da's. We put the saddle down to its lowest but you still couldn't reach the pedals so you had to cycle standing up. It wasn't that hard, but you had to be careful you didn't bang your balls off the crossbar.

Everyone brought their schoolbag with picnic stuff and lemonade. Someone said we'd stop halfway at Dublin Airport to eat our sandwich. I don't think anyone can have looked at a map because it took another four hours to get to Drogheda, even though we had a gale force wind behind us. The head was OK, a skull with bits of black skin on it, not that scary, but it was a long way to go to see a relic.

We had Lawrence O'Toole's finger in our church and you could see that any day of the week. At least you wouldn't be exhausted and hardly able to walk or kneel down to say a prayer. Sometimes when we got new altar boys to train in, we'd give them the job of putting out all the candles and lights in the church. We'd make sure they ended up at the side altar where the finger was. When it was finally pitch dark everywhere we'd switch on the light in the finger box. It was so long and bony and always seemed to be pointing straight at you, that one of the new boys fainted and we were barred from doing it again and Father McOrly made us wash and polish his car inside and out that Saturday.

The way home was a nightmare. The rain started lashing and the gale blew it straight into our faces. Da's bike was really heavy. I knew I was great at the running, but you use different muscles on a bike. I was a bit behind the others and decided to sprint to catch up. But my foot slipped on the pedal and I hit my balls a terrible belt off the crossbar. I nearly fell off with the pain and had to stop. Kevin O'Farrell had longer legs than anyone so we swapped bikes. But it wasn't long before his balls got a terrible belt as well. There was no chance any of the others would swap bikes now. So him and me kept switching over, and every time it happened you just had to get off and push the bike along until the pain went away.

The other lads weren't much better because their bums were torn to shreds from sitting on their wet saddles. Everyone was cursing and blaming each other for not checking how many miles it would take to see that poxy head. It was a terrible experience and everyone swore they'd never cycle again. There was a lot of Germolene bought off Mr Stanley our chemist that week. Lying in bed that night I was still sore and very glad that Shea had stopped wetting the bed. But I still would have liked to have bought that red bike.

It only took a week to forget about Finch. Da came home in great form on Thursday evening in his boss's black Citroën. He told me to finish my bread and jam as fast as I could because he had a big surprise for me. It was still really bright and sunny at seven o'clock when we both got into the car. My pals were raging as me and Da drove off on our own for once and headed down the street, and he never went up on the path once as we turned into Seville Place. I was sure he was bringing me to visit his ma. Everyone said she was a lovely granny, and she lived in Clontarf, but I thought she was a bit severe and I didn't like the way she talked to Da about his drinking when we'd go to visit her on Friday nights, and there was always a smell of mothballs and peppermint off her, and I'd always have to go into the kitchen and eat the Marietta biscuits she'd leave out for me when she was having her secret talk with Da. My Uncle Paul lived with her and he had his own grocer's shop on the North Strand and was really rich, so you'd think they'd have at least chocolate Goldgrain, but thank God we passed the end of their road at Clontarf and Da said we were heading for Dollymount, my favourite place in the whole world.

It was just starting to rain. The wind was blowing the sand everywhere. The tide was out so there was hardly anyone on the beach. Just a man leaning into the wind with his black umbrella, holding a woman's hand, so they mustn't have got married yet. Da tooted the horn and then I waved. Then they stopped holding hands. Da laughed when I asked him did he know them and stopped the car. Da broke into hysterics when they started running away from us down the beach. Then he got out and told me to get into the driver's seat. He pulled it forward and took two cushions from the back of the car and put them under me and started to teach me how to drive.

It was so easy. I couldn't believe it. The hardest part was stretching my feet to reach the pedals. He told me I was a natural – up and down the strand, fast twists, screeching to a stop, handbrake turns, everything. He even got out and let me have a go on my own. There was another car coming towards me. I wanted to show off so I raced straight towards them and they had to swerve at the last minute and I could see Da with his hands on his head. He must have been trying to keep his hat on his head with the wind. All the seagulls kept flying out of the way at the last minute. It was the best start to a holiday I ever had.

After a while I knew Da thought I was doing a good job because he was bathing his feet in the water and looking across at Howth Head and not holding onto his cap any more. I swished by him in the shallow water and splashed him, so he waved at me to stop. I did a wheelie with the handbrake. His eyes were twinkling bright blue when he got into the passenger seat in his bare feet carrying his shoes. He'd got a great idea. I was allowed drive the car back across Dollymount bridge but not onto the main road. He got me to slide right down beneath the dashboard and just work the pedals. He sat up straight in the passenger seat with his right hand low on the steering wheel – it looked like nobody was driving the car. Da would tell me to slow down any time there was a car coming towards us. I never heard him laugh so much when he'd tell me the look on the other drivers' faces, but we had to stop when one of them nearly crashed.

When we got onto the main road he took over again and all the way home he told me about him being the chief test mechanic in the Irish Grand Prix in the Phoenix Park. That's when I decided I'd become a racing driver and make him really proud of me, and even though I really wanted to, I never told him my plan about never ever going back to school. Even though he never asked me not to, I never told Ma anything about the mad night we had, although when I went to bed that night and shoved Shea over to his own side, I could hear them laughing downstairs and there wasn't even one row so he must have told Ma something about it.

No matter who Dublin were playing against it didn't matter because I always knew who to cheer for. Especially when they were playing Meath. Everyone in our parish, even the mas and das, hated Meath. There was probably some nice people from there but the moneylender in our parish who used to stop the dockers on their way home on their bikes on payday on Thursday night was from Meath, and Mr O'Farrell – who I always thought was a very nice man – was from Meath as well and maybe that's why nobody liked him. But when Wexford were playing Tipperary, it was always a big problem for me. Ma and Uncle Mick were both from Wexford and when they were in the final, loads of cousins and uncles would come up from Enniscorthy and stay with us. You'd be praying they'd win because they'd give you their Wexford hats and purple and gold rosettes and loads of money. We were never that close to my da's family but my da's grandfather Arthur had won two All Irelands playing in goal for Tipperary, and I always wanted to be like him.

That year after my head accident Wexford were playing Tipperary in a very important match, and the nice man from Croke Park had sent me the two tickets so I gave them to Ma and Da. I don't think they'd ever gone to a match together. I think Ma was a bit annoyed with Da about something and Wexford were favourites so she was determined to go. It was summer and the farmers in Wexford were saving the hay or the lambs or something so none of Ma's relations came up. I watched them walking down Emerald Street alone together, the first time I'd ever seen it, and I hoped they'd hold hands like the man and the woman in Dollymount with the umbrella. But it was raining and they didn't.

Uncle Mick was listening to the match on the wireless and he had his pencil and cardboard from the cornflakes ready. I knew he'd be cheering for Wexford so I wasn't going to listen with him. I grabbed the stolen transistor that Tommy was minding for Michael Carney, and took Bobby out for a walk to Fairview. When we were going by the North Strand, you could hear the roar of the Croke Park crowd. I kept flicking the transistor switch on and off real quick. Wexford were winning by a mile, but they had a strong wind behind them in the first half. Me and Bobby sat down in the sun near the flowers in Fairview Park. At least they were up there together, but I didn't want either of them to be sad. I kept watching the clock on the pub across the road because I knew it would be over at ten to five. I heard a huge last roar and switched on the transistor. Tipperary had won by a point. All the way home the Tipperary people in their blue and gold were teeming out of Croke Park heading for the train and roaring with delight. I felt terrible sorry for Ma, but I needn't have worried. Da did a fantastic thing that night.

He hadn't spent all his bonus – that he thought we didn't know about and that I finally remembered to look up in the dictionary – and he brought Ma to the Royal where Joseph Locke was singing. He even brought her into the Gresham Hotel. He had a pint and Ma had an Irish coffee. I knew because I heard her telling her best friend Theresa about it and that at long last, Jimmy seemed to be slowing down a bit on the drink, only the odd binge, and maybe she could persuade him to go to the doctor about the pain in his stomach.

Uncle Mick was giving out like hell about the referee but he was muttering that at least now that Wexford were out of it, the hay would be saved in Wexford and people hadn't wasted their time coming up to see a farce of a fiasco and Tipperary would get their comeuppance anyway if they came up against Cork and Christy Ring.

The next day was a disaster. It must have been one of Da's binge days that I'd heard Ma telling Theresa about. Ma had taken Elaine up to the nuns in Eccles Street to get her entered into the music school. Tommy was off on an excursion to Bohernabreena with his gang, and there was no way he'd take me. Shea and Mary Joe were staying with my cousins in Marino where Auntie Bridie would give you Bovril before going to bed, so I was left in charge of the whole house and Uncle Mick all on my own.

Uncle Mick was getting a bit doddery and couldn't even boil an egg. I did my best but he said it was too runny and gave me money to buy him and me chips. Ma never would let him eat chips because it was bad for his circulation, and we were all warned never to buy him chewing tobacco. But that's what he wanted so I couldn't refuse, specially when he gave me a tanner for myself and to say nothing to Ma. Then old Mrs Lacey next door asked me to get her a small baby Powers whiskey in the Ball Alley and gave me another tanner for myself. It looked like I nearly had the price of a bike from the police auction, but then disaster struck. I was just washing Uncle Mick's plate in the cold water when I heard the screech of the brakes.

I knew Da's knock before he fell in the door, and when

I saw which black Citroën was outside I was certain he'd had a go at the Archbishop's whiskey. I tried to give Da Uncle Mick's runny egg in the parlour 'cos I didn't want Uncle Mick to see him like this, but it nearly made him sick. He was muttering, 'I'm just going to bed for a little snooze, say nothing to Ma.' Then something else as I pulled the blankets over him. I could barely hear him.

'What's that, Da?'

'It's very important, son. Can't find . . . Where's the keys . . . Got to – got to – wake me at five, got to get the car back – got to . . .' Then a few little prayers, Hail Mary, Holy Mary, then a few gentle snores.

Outside the street was empty. At least no one had seen him staggering in. But the car was parked about four feet from the kerb and very crooked. The driver's door wasn't locked, so I got in. There was a lovely leather smell off the seats but I could still smell Da, and he'd left the keys in the ignition. I had to have a go. Switching it on was easy and after all my practice on Dollymount Strand I got it into first gear. I pretended I was the Archbishop going to a wedding or a funeral, or even a confirmation, and said the 'Confiteor' out loud in Latin. I drove it down the street a bit and swung it close to the kerb with only one wheel on the path. It was outside Granny Wilson's house but there was no sign of her, maybe she was having a little snooze too. I was surprised there wasn't any holy water or extreme unction oil anywhere that I could anoint Da with to make him sober, but sure enough, I did find the bottle of whiskey and it was nearly all gone.

'Da – Da – it's half five, you've got to get the car back.' It never happened before. He shoulda stuck to the Guinness.

'Please Da, you'll lose your job. Ma'll go mad.' He looked so peaceful, I knew he'd never wake up in time.

Or maybe 'cos I wanted to do something special for him. Anyway I tiptoed down the stairs past Uncle Mick chewing away on his forbidden tobacco and out on the sunny street. There was no one around. Granny Wilson must have been listening to the election stuff on the wireless. Mr DeValera had been voted back in. Uncle Mick had been listening to it all day, but he must have been up for the other crowd because he was chewing and muttering away to himself. Anyway no one saw me sneak into the car, start it up quietly and cruise down Emerald Street and around the corner.

The traffic home from the docks hadn't really started yet and Sheriff Street was still quiet. Just a coalman on his horse and cart and a few men on bicycles. There was no one coming the other way so I drove on the wrong side of the road for a while 'cos it was safer. Then a stupid oul wan with a shopping bag stepped out. I could see her terrified eyes as I barely missed her and could hear her bad language through the open window as I screeched by. I was very surprised − Ma never cursed even when she was really annoyed. I pulled in for a while to let a big truck go by. I could see my friend Kevin O'Farrell's red hair in the mirror. He was going up to Tara Street baths for a swim. His ma always made him do that, even though it was full of oul fellas at six o'clock. He nearly died when I bipped the horn at him. When I told him, he said I was mad, but he still got in. There was an awful lot of traffic in Amiens Street so I had to drive on the path for a while, and nearly hit a bus stop. But no one in the queue cursed at us, or maybe we didn't hear them because we were gone by so fast. We were nearly at Store Street where my da's garage was when I remembered there was a police station on the corner, and sure enough there were two huge Guards standing at the corner having a smoke. I parked half on the path.

Kevin didn't want to do it, but finally he went over to distract them and told them there was an oul fella with his thing out waving it at kids in Gardener Street, and they were gone like lightning. I don't know how I got across all the traffic, especially the buses, but thank God there was a big empty space outside the garage because Da hadn't taught me parking yet and anyway I was getting a terrible headache.

Just when I was getting out I saw a book on the back leather seat about Matt Talbot. He used to be a terrible drinker until one day when he had no money left he was standing outside Cusack's pub on the North Strand and all his pals went by, never asking him if he had a tongue on him, I think that's what Da told me. Anyway he went straight up to the Jesuits in Gardener Street and took the pledge and never touched another drop and now they were going to make a saint out of him. Maybe the Archbishop had the same problem as Da, if he was reading that book, but Da needed it more so I took it with me, and it wasn't really stealing 'cos it was in such a good cause.

Barney the foreman wasn't a bit surprised when I gave him the keys and told him Da'd had to slip into Molloy's for an urgent message. Kevin was off up in Gardener Street with the two huge Gardaí looking for the man with his thing out and I hoped he wouldn't get into trouble, so I ran straight home. There was a huge crowd in Emerald Street when I got back, women and kids and Da sitting on the kerb with his head in his hands.

Later that night we went for our walk, Da had calmed down and stopped giving out to me, and even though it was the worst fright he'd got in a long time he promised me he'd read the Matt Talbot book and for the first time ever he gave me two shillings and it wasn't even payday. Kevin O' Farrell didn't talk to me for nearly a week and

David Casey told me he'd seen him being brought home in a squad car.

Da would never break his word. He read the Matt Talbot book from cover to cover, sitting in his chair in the kitchen. He was never a great reader, just the evening paper or the *Ireland's Own* magazine, but he had great handwriting. He sent me a letter once when he had to go to England to learn about the new Citroëns with hydraulic suspensions and even grey and white colours as well as the black. The day he was coming home I stood on the bridge where we used to watch the trains shunting, and watched every aeroplane that flew over and wondered which one he was on. Ma had great hopes that he might have another go at the pledge when she saw him reading the book, but when he got to the part about the chains he changed his mind completely and went out for a pint.

Uncle Mick had given up the drink years ago so he never read the book. He thought Matt Talbot was a bit of a scab for working through the Great Strike. When my brother Shea heard the story from Da he decided he was going to be a saint, but Ma wouldn't let him wear the chains. So he did the fasting thing where you're only allowed to have tea and toast and no sugar. My Auntie Chrissie's boyfriend Andy used to bring us down loads of sweets and Shea got fed up looking at me eating his share, so he gave the whole thing up after a week. When Kevin O'Farrell was back talking to me it must have had a big effect on him because he started to go to seven o'clock mass every morning, and sure enough there was soon loads of priests calling in to their house again. I'd never seen Da laugh so much when I told him. 'Sure isn't it better than having the Guards calling around,' he said.

I didn't know it was going to be my last Sunday at home for a long time and even if I did I'd have done the same thing. I loved the picnics in Dollymount even though I had to walk out because the conductor was fed up with Bobby puking upstairs in the bus, despite not feeding him all day Saturday, and so they wouldn't let Bobby on any more. But once I got to Fairview Park I could let Bobby off the lead because he used to nearly pull my right arm out of my socket and even back then everyone said I'd a very strong handshake. But once we turned around the bend there at Clontarf you could see the wooden bridge at Dollymount and the Hill of Howth beyond, and you'd think Bobby knew, because he'd take off like a rocket and wait patiently for me at the bridge. It was still a long walk to the picnic spot and Da would always be there before me with the kettle already on the fire. We'd sit on the little sandhill and watch the golfers, hoping they'd miss one and send it towards us, and we'd listen to the kettle singing in the heat and Da would stub out his cigarette to keep it for later, and gaze across at Howth. He said I should buy a house there someday.

'I will, Da, I will.' Because I'd seen the very one I wanted for us.

'No not that one, Da. The one looking down on the lighthouse, the big white one.'

Da put on his glasses. 'Your grandfather used to drive the Howth train.'

'You could even grow strawberries there and sell them, Da. It's always sunny in Howth.'

He'd never look at me when he'd ask me a hard question.

'Are you all right now, son? Your mother's worried about you.'

'You mean the head thing? Da, I told you already, I just know sometimes when things are going to happen.' Da lit up the rest of his fag.

'There's nothing wrong with that, Robbie, nothing at all.' He stood on the sandhill looking over at Howth.

'You're right, son, it's a lovely house.' He just kept staring, for a long time, across the sea at the house on the hill.

I knew there was something serious going on when I saw Ma and Elaine were tidying up the parlour one day and shining up the brass fender around the fireplace. It wasn't even near Christmas, so maybe there was a priest calling. But it wasn't that either because everyone else was sent out to our cousins' except me and I was told to put on my confirmation coat and shoes and wait in the kitchen. Uncle Mick was reading the death notices in the paper, and Bobby had been put in the yard, so I knew Ma must have been expecting men visitors. I sneaked up to my bedroom to peep out the window and didn't put on the light. Two men were getting out of the car. I recognised Mr McIvor, the head man, straight away. The other one was a doctor too because he had a black case. I had to come down to listen, but the parlour door was much thicker than the kitchen one so you could barely hear a thing. But I did recognise Da's voice and if he was in there as well, it could only be bad news. I don't know why Ma made me put on the suit because neither me or Bobby ever got to see any doctors that night.

The next day everyone was really nice to me and I got extra ice cream, so I was scared as hell about what was going on in the parlour the night before. Da came home with a brand new racing bicycle with red tape on the handlebars and a silver slipstream front light, with a silver dynamo on the back wheel and a silver horn with a black button taped to the left handlebar near the five-speed gear lever. It was magical. I knew Da didn't have the money to buy it and I saw the hire purchase docket from McHughes' posh bicycle shop in Talbot Street. I kept thinking I must have leukaemia or something worse, but how would an eye man know that? I had to pretend to Da I was delighted and took it out for a drive. It was incredible, it went so fast and smooth. All the kids on the street wanted a go and I let them. Everyone said how lucky I was. Then my Uncle Nicky came down and gave me five bob for myself and rubbed my hair. Jesus, I was in big trouble. When I put the bike carefully in the back kitchen, Uncle Nicky was in the parlour talking to Ma and I was afraid to listen.

I sneaked Bobby out and we went for a walk out to Fairview Park. Even Bobby must have known that something was wrong, because he never left my side for a second, and when we lay down to watch the big men playing soccer up on the hill near the railway line he never chased the ball, just sat there beside me licking my hand. We walked home in the dark the other way, the East Wall way, and Bobby never pulled on the lead once. When we were nearly at the bridge where me and Da used to watch the trains shunting, I saw a man in the distance leaning against the wall, smoking. Bobby knew immediately. I didn't notice till we got nearer.

'There you are, son, I was looking for you.' We sat on the wall and chatted for a long time. All the usual stuff about the stars, how far away they are, how you'd never know if they were still there or not. He never mentioned my new red bicycle and neither did I. He was a terrible man for bad news. All he could say was, 'Robbie, sometimes we have to do things in life that we don't really want to, but only if it's for the best.' He was staring up at the Dublin mountains and it was the first time ever I saw tears in his eyes. I couldn't bear it so I just said, 'We're still buying that big white house in Howth, aren't we, Da?'

He was looking up at the night sky. 'If there's a God in heaven, son, you'll buy that house!'

Tommy was still being nice the next day. He even poured milk on my cornflakes that morning and lent me his leather jacket until dinnertime. Ma, as usual, broke the bad news.

'It's only for observation. Maybe only two weeks.'

But I knew if they got their hands on me they'd never let me go.

For the first time ever I wished my schoolbag was bigger. Everyone was out so I knew it was safe. Da was in Noctor's and Shea was playing cricket in Fairview Park. My sisters were doing Irish dancing in McGann's and Ma had gone into town to buy me new pyjamas and I'd seen Tommy heading off holding Hattie Hobson's hand. That's when I decided to take his new leather jacket with me.

The hardest part was saying goodbye to Bobby – but I couldn't delay because I knew the ship that Mr Brown drove left at four o'clock. I was hoping it would go somewhere sunny like Brazil, for the football, but anywhere would do and anyway Mr Brown always took loads of sandwiches with him so it must be somewhere far.

Saturday was always a quiet day on the docks. I hid behind the creosote logs for ages until I saw Mr Brown go into the cabin to change into his yellow oilskins. He always did that. He was a terrible nice man and never gave out about us playing football on the street, and his oldest son Liam was the spit of Elvis Presley according to my sister Elaine. I knew I'd miss my baby sister Mary Joe the most and couldn't believe I'd forgotten to leave her a note. The other man that travelled all over the world with Mr Brown was baldy and thank God wore corporation glasses so I knew he couldn't see far. He'd loosened the ropes and the engine was chugging and I was running and I never once doubted I'd make the jump. They were up in the cabin now and chatting away as the ship slipped past the Poolbeg lighthouse.

I didn't start to cry until we were passing the Baily lighthouse and Howth. I began to think of my da and how much he'd miss me, and my ma doing the best for all of us, and sitting up in bed all night coughing with her asthma and knitting us jumpers, and it started to rain and even Tommy's leather jacket wouldn't cover me. I was getting soaked and freezing.

Mr Brown never gave out one bit to me and just listened when I told him about the hospital. It was really warm in the cabin and he poured me a cup of hot cocoa from the flask, and said he'd have me home in three hours, they just had to tow a boat in.

When I got home I should have guessed that Ma was lying about the 'just two weeks' because she never said a word about me being missing and was washing and ironing nearly all of my clothes. Even Tommy never said anything about the rip in his new leather jacket.

PART II

'WHAT'S AN ORTHOPAEDIC hospital, Ma?' We were on the bus to Castle Avenue where the hospital was but I couldn't spot any castles, even at the terminus. Auntie Chrissie was carrying my big case and she told me she knew some of the nurses there and they were all very nice. We walked in through the huge gates, between two statues of women with not very much clothes on, holding lanterns over their heads. It was really sunny and hot and I should have been playing football in Fairview Park. It wasn't even a castle either, more like a big mansion. There was fourteen steps up to the big yellow door. The windows were huge and pointy at the top and I could see two boys with white faces staring out of a third-floor window. I wondered if Ma or Chrissie could smell the fear or was it only Da that could do that.

All the corridors were shiny and polished and the big stairs and banisters wound all the way up to the top. But there was no kids anywhere. Just wards full of babies that smelled like they'd all wet their beds.

The Matron took my case. She seemed nice enough but she got a nurse to take me up to the top floor before I could say a proper goodbye. The ward she took me into was big and brown and old with beds and kids and a few stretchers all around, but at least there was no smell. She put my big case on a bed in the middle and told me to

113

wave goodbye to Ma. I ran to the window and saw Auntie Chrissie with her arm around Ma, disappearing between the big hedges in the sun.

There was a grey steel locker beside my bed, and loads of boys way younger than Shea – all on crutches and even one with just one arm – crowded around me, asking me what I was in for and had I any sweets in my big case. There was a wireless blaring at the end of the ward, and two nurses listening to the horse show. It was nearly over and they cheered when Ireland won the Aga Khan Cup and ran straight out of the ward. One of them looked really nice and I hoped she was one of Aunt Chrissie's friends.

All the kids were wearing grey jackets and grey short trousers, except one. A boy called Jim Clancy, who was much bigger than me, who had just come in on his crutches and was wearing long ones. He let me feel the long iron rods inside them and told me they were callipers. He explained everything to me. It was the polio and thalidomide ward for up to sevens, but they always put the new boys up here for a few weeks and he was just visiting a friend, but much better if I could get down to the veranda where he and all the older boys lived, near the orchard, and you could see the lights of the buses going by at night-time in the distance. And the doors opened out and you could see right into the girls' ward where Jim Clancy's girlfriend was. She had a bad muscle thing and neither of them were allowed run. But there was an empty space down there because his other friend Michael Porter had gone to Cherry Orchard Hospital with the scarlet fever, and I should ask Sister Conroy because she got on very well with Matron and do it straight away or they'd forget about me and leave me up here forever.

Sister Conroy was very surprised to see me standing

there in her office with my brown case and still in my street clothes. She looked like Aunt Chrissie and had the same smile. She couldn't find my file and laughed and wondered was I in the right hospital and so did I. Thank God she said I was old enough for long trousers, because all the other boys on the veranda wore them and that's where I was to go. She smiled again when I told her I'd already had a bath and she told the nurse that another one wouldn't do me any harm and to scrub behind my ears. The nurse was too young and wouldn't turn away when I was taking off my clothes and I wasn't surprised to find out later that she was from County Meath. I was so embarrassed but at least she left me alone to dress myself after the bath. I had a good look in the huge mirror. All the mirrors at home were tiny and anyway there was always someone around and I stared at my reflection for a long time.

It wasn't gonna be easy to cure them all. There were twelve on the boys' side even before I could think about the girls' ward and I probably wouldn't even be allowed in there and anyway Ma said just two weeks. Some of the boys were very old and my best friend Jim Clancy said two of them even had pubic hair. I pretended not to be surprised even though I knew only girls got them. Shea had finally told me what it looked like when they pulled down Lily Downey's knickers. He'd waited until the morning I was going into hospital. He'd heard there was girls in there and didn't want me to get the shock of my life like what happened to him. But Jim Clancy was right because that very night one of the older ones that was bedridden asked me to get him a bed bottle and he let me watch him pissing, and there was loads of hair. He had polio and one of his legs was very skinny but his thing was big enough.

The next morning I had another good look in the huge bathroom mirror and sure enough I discovered two hairs. That was the most important day of my life so far but not because of the two hairs. It was my first full day on the veranda and I was getting to know most of the lads. The nurse from Meath that gave me the bath said I was a bit small and skinny for my age but at least I could run and play relievio and there was nothing wrong with me even though I was the only one that knew that. When some of the boys asked me what I was in for I just said observation and left it at that.

There was one boy, Richard Mooney. He was a thalidomider. I never saw anyone like him. He had no hands because he had no arms, just a finger coming out of his shoulder and very friendly. When he saw my deck of cards he wanted a game. We started pontoon, he called it twenty-one. I knew I was brilliant at that 'cos Da had taught me how to remember all the cards and you're not allowed shuffle. We weren't even playing for money. I was sitting on his bed and he said he wanted to be dealer. Next thing, he picked up the cards and started dealing with his toes. Nobody else seemed to notice but I couldn't believe it. Then he'd hold his cards between his chin and his one and only finger. I was so amazed I lost every single game. He was laughing all the time in a nice way until he suddenly stopped. He was looking at someone behind me and I could tell by his face it wasn't good news.

'Shove up in the bed, Mooney. I want to show the new chap a card trick.' His name was Tommy Lyons and two of the nurses fancied him. He was the other one with pubic hair, in for multiple sclerosis or something. He picked up the cards.

'I hear you're in for observation.' A lot of the other lads had moved closer. 'Well observe this – it's called 52 pick-up' and he flung the full deck of cards all over the floor, under the beds, everywhere, then nearly creased himself laughing. All the others joined in except Jim Clancy and Richard Mooney.

That's when I knew it was the most important day in my life so far, apart from the Croke Park thing and I remembered about being fearless and although it was only my second fight ever and he was fifteen, I nearly killed him stone dead. I was across the locker fast and hit him two punches and had him on the floor in a headlock and kneed him in the balls and I wouldn't let him go till a nurse pulled me off him. It must have been one of the ones that fancied him because she kept pulling my hair till I let him go and she went straight to Sister Conroy. That was the worst part because Sister Conroy said I'd let her down. Even the Matron was told, and for punishment I was sent back up to the mansion for a week into the babies' ward.

The best part was my pal Jim Clancy calling up to see me and telling me I was the hero of the veranda, and that none of them were afraid of more Tommy Lyons any more, and I could be the true leader when I came back down. Even Richard Mooney sent up two packets of crisps and a note that he wrote with his feet saying he heard Sister Conroy telling Nurse Feeney that they'd only leave me up there for one night and that Tommy Lyons had been getting too big for his boots anyway, and Jim Clancy said he thought Nurse Feeney fancied me and wanted to get off her mark with me. I didn't want to pretend to Jim Clancy that I was interested, but I was hoping Nurse Feeney was the one in the girls' ward with the green eyes and long black hair.

But I didn't forget my real job so when all the nurses were gone that night I went round all the babies and put my hands on their heads and bar one they didn't hardly cry the whole night long.

Next day back on the veranda me and Tommy Lyons shook hands. He was limping a bit and his black eye was bigger than mine. He gave me two dirty postcards of nude girls to keep and I lent him my harmonica until twenty past six. Shea was right. They grew hair down there as well. It was very stormy that night and I told Richard Mooney and Jim Clancy a ghost story before they fell asleep.

The trees outside were swaying like mad and dark spattered rain blew against the veranda windows. Way to my right in the distance I could see the night-duty nurse in her little office with the neon lights, jiving to the music that I could just barely hear, and blowing smoke rings in the air. It sounded like Buddy Holly and she was fixing her hair just like my sister Elaine. Thirteen boys to her right and twenty girls to her left. I was wondering was Jim Clancy's girlfriend still awake like me or maybe dreaming of having a walk with him without falling over or needing crutches. The jiving changed to a slow dance. It was definitely Buddy Holly. I could hear it clearly now – 'True Love Ways' – and I remembered my promise to God. Twelve sleeping boys, six to my right, six to my left. If I could really believe, maybe I could cure them all. I jumped out of bed and dressed quietly. The night nurse was dancing faster and faster to a new Buddy Holly song, 'Rave On'. I knew it and could remember all the words. I stepped outside into the wind and rain and cold and walked towards the huge trees that looked like giants in the dark, and I hoped He could hear me as I shouted my prayers to God against the roar of the wind that blew across the city and the park.

The food was terrible. Breakfast was OK – milk in a tin cup and as much bread and butter as you wanted. But dinner was poxy. They called it lunch but no matter what name they put on it you couldn't eat it. The meat was even gristlier than in my penpal's house in Nobber, and always tapioca afterwards that was so lumpy you'd vomit. They'd go berserk if you didn't eat it all and threaten you with the baby ward. But Richard Mooney was a brilliant pal and he'd eat all my stuff to keep me out of trouble, and he never even got fat. But even he couldn't stick all the tapioca and one day he said that was it – he couldn't stomach another bite. Then my best friend Jim Clancy gave me a brilliant idea. They used to take your temperature every day at twelve and if it was over two hundred, I think he said, they'd mark you down as sick, and you'd be allowed take an extra book from the library every day, and they'd give you jelly and ice cream after the gristle. That's when I started running.

The playground was square and was about a hundred steps each side. I'd start about ten in the morning and do lap after lap and I wouldn't stop until about ten to twelve. Then I'd wait to get my breath back before they came around. It always worked perfect. I'd say I did it ten times in those first two weeks and I had them all worried, even Sister Conroy, that I'd got the scarlet fever.

I must have read all the Agatha Christie books they had in the library and I was almost getting sick of the jelly and ice cream when they copped on to what was happening, but then one great thing happened. My best friend Jim Clancy used to count how many laps I'd do and he asked me quietly when we were in our beds one night, did I think there was a chance that he ever could run. By this stage I'd done so many cures that I knew it worked quicker if they asked you themselves. And when he said it was the one thing in his whole life he'd love to be able to do, I knew I could cure him.

We started early the next morning. It was dark and

the night nurses were still on but I thought it was best if no one saw us. I ran beside him at first and he was using both crutches, but it was very slow. After twenty-three laps it was getting a bit brighter and you could see the early morning buses passing by and that's when he threw away one crutch and did a whole lap before he fell.

The next morning he was a bit nervous but he got five done on one crutch and I could see by his face that he was ready and he threw the other one away and leant on me and kept going. I didn't have to say anything but I knew when he was going to do it and he did. He ran the whole length of one of the sides on his own, without crutches, and grabbed the wire fence at the far end near the trees. He started crying then but I knew he was cured. Early next morning when he called me I pretended to be asleep so he went on his own. It was pissing rain but he did it – three laps without falling over and he never even brought the crutches, and I saw his girlfriend sneak over and kiss him in the rain. After that he even did the jelly-and-ice-cream trick and it worked better for him 'cos there was no way they thought he could run.

You'd hardly believe they only allowed visitors in once a week, on Sundays from two to four. They made sure you wouldn't complain about the food because they gave you a fry for breakfast after mass in the gym and meat you could eat for your dinner and I couldn't believe when Da was first in to visit that I'd barely thought about him all week, but there was a lot going on. The minute I saw him I wanted to hug him and get him to take me home. Everyone I knew came to see me that first Sunday, even Uncle Mick whose arthritis was completely gone since they threatened him with extreme unction. Some of the lads had no visitors at all because their people were from miles away, like Trim and Castledermot. Ma was great. She went along them all and had a chat with them but she gave away too many of my sweets. I asked her twice to find out from the Matron when they were going to start observing my head but she said those things were better left to the doctors and Da said he agreed. She didn't answer when I asked her what day she'd be collecting me next week. Everyone was chatting and laughing but I think she heard. Whatever was going on, I knew then I wouldn't be going home for a long time.

Jim Clancy was right. Nurse Feeney did fancy me and she was the black-haired beautiful nurse with the green eyes that I'd hoped. How I found out was one night she was on duty with Nurse Bannister. Nurse Bannister had huge diddies and she'd let the older boys feel them sometimes, but only from the outside. I'd never do that, especially when Nurse Feeney was around. One night the two of them were whispering in the dark. They were right at the end of my bed and must have thought I was asleep.

'His mother is so elegant. I'd say she was a real beauty in her day,' Nurse Bannister whispered. 'I think his father is the spit of Clark Gable.' Then Nurse Feeney's soft velvet voice. 'He's the image of his da. I wonder what he's in for – there's nothing wrong with him.'

I couldn't sleep the whole night and wanted to write her a love letter but I couldn't find a pencil but just as well because when I told Jim Clancy the next day he said I'd done the right thing and let her make the first move. He was right and I didn't have to wait long.

'Quick Robbie, quick! Wake up. The rabbit . . . Someone let him out of the hutch. Put on your clothes.' The first time Nurse Feeney had ever used my name. Maybe it was a dream, but when I opened my eyes, she was standing at my locker handing me my clothes. She went outside the veranda and stood shivering in the rain until I was dressed. I wouldn't let her down! A memory forever – running through the bushes, the wet leaves on my face, over the wire fence and down the muddy track – then the dark lane by the park and Nurse Feeney's shouts of warning not far behind. Running as fast as I could, then the sudden stop, the rabbit in the car's headlights, then the crash, the fur and blood. God, fix him if you can! My hands on fire as I pick him up, the bleeding stops, just the rabbit's frightened stare – thank God, thank God.

Back inside the hutch, the rabbit munches safely. Nurse Feeney holds my hand – such a soft hand – then that gentle kiss that lasts forever. Is it real or is it just a dream? But she's gone now, a shadow in the rain. I walk and run and walk, looking for someone to tell my story to, someone to make it real.

Derek was the only boy awake when I got back. He was my next best pal after Jim Clancy. He had dark curly hair and a big smile, but he was bedridden with the haemophilia – a terrible thing because if you bumped into him or he cut himself he could bleed to death. I knew I'd have a lot to do and an awful lot more practice before I could cure anything as big as that, but at least I could be his eyes and legs while he was stuck in the ward.

Every single night I'd sit on his bed and tell him all about the day. He loved the stories about the flour attacks on the girls' ward, but his favourite was when we'd rob the orchards in some of the posh gardens in Clontarf and get chased. He'd laugh so much I'd get terrified he'd fall out of the bed and do himself an injury and maybe bleed to death. He was a great poet and a joker and could make up brilliant songs and limericks of everything we told him.

But that night when just the two of us were awake, I told him the story about Nurse Feeney and the rabbit and the kiss. I swore him to secrecy and he vowed he'd never tell anyone, not even his ma or da. I could see by his big bright eyes that he'd love a girlfriend too. So I promised him I'd fix him up with my younger sister Mary Joe, who'd never even had one boyfriend yet, and was really beautiful and would be perfect for him.

His ma always brought me in some sweets for looking after him, nearly always Scots Clan, and his da would stand and shake my hand each Sunday as he left. But he didn't get to meet my sister Mary Joe. I never knew what happened when he died. No cuts, no bruises 'cos I'd sneaked a peep inside the screen. My first dead person. I didn't cry, not then, but later when his da gave me his cards and draughts, a shoe box full of toys and a picture of a boy and girl dancing around a Halloween bonfire. They were holding hands and there was writing above the heads saying Derek loves Mary Joe. When his da shook my hand for that last time, I saw the saddest question in his eyes.

He didn't know, no more than me, why Derek died.

Halloween in the hospital was the worst day ever. They wouldn't let you dress up. You'd get monkey nuts OK, but there was no colcannon. The day nurses would get ready for their parties and let you paint moustaches on them because they'd all go as men, or doctors, but once they headed off, the night nurses would be in such a temper at having to work that they'd make us all go to bed early and put out the lights. A lot of the boys were in hospital so long they didn't even know what Halloween was, and what they were missing. But me and Jim Clancy did. We waited until everyone was asleep and the night nurses were having their wine. Nobody saw us crossing the playground in the dark. He brought his crutches just in case but didn't need that much help climbing over the fence to cross the orchard and the field. We just sat near the hedge beside the road, watching the buses going into town with people dressed up as witches and pirates. We could see the glow of the bonfires in the distance and hear the fireworks from somewhere far away. It was all a bit sad so we just went back and went straight to bed.

I think he fell asleep straight away, but I just lay there and thought about Emerald Street and my pals, and wondered what I was missing. Da used to let us have all the old tyres he couldn't sell for our bonfire in the lane in Oriel Street. Clicky Kelly's gang would always have a much bigger one than ours because they'd rob a whole car and throw it on top, but we'd never do that. The East Wallers always had the best one in our parish. They'd steal loads of wood from the timber factory, in T.C. Martin's or Brook Thomas's, and wooden pallets from Dolan's the fruit warehouse. When our bonfire was gone out, we'd race down there because they weren't as dangerous as Clicky Kelly's gang and wouldn't attack you, or throw burning tyres at you, only steal your football. They were a bit older than us and always had loads of girls that wanted a chase. Some of them would let the boys catch them on purpose and pretend they were afraid they were going to be thrown on the bonfire. They'd have to beg for mercy and do a forfeit, like kiss somebody. I was dying to be asked because I'd learned a good bit about all that stuff from Hattie Hobson and the girl from Tramore but I was never picked. But at least Halloween was the one day of the year Ma would let us stay out as long as we wanted, other than Christmas Day.

I knew no matter what happened I'd be out for Christmas. To cheer myself up I lay in bed that lousy Halloween night thinking of every minute of that last Christmas at home. I'd got a new torch — a big rubber one that could shine up on to the clouds at night-time. It was snowing all that day and everything was white and magical and thank God for that because it was the first year I didn't believe in Santy any more. I remembered finding the cowboy suit that I'd written to Santy about in Uncle Mick's cupboard when I was trying to find Elaine's golliwog, and my worst fears had come true.

No matter how much Ma and Da tried to persuade me that a cowboy suit would be great, I kept telling them that I'd gone off the whole idea and wrote to Santy about getting a big torch. Shea was thrilled when he got the cowboy suit even though he hadn't asked for one and I loved my torch.

Then the night nurses came around to give out the medicine. I was having such great memories of being back home, I just swallowed it without pretending to wake up. Having that torch was like being a detective. I could shine it on the back windows of the houses in Oriel Street, when everyone in our house was asleep and I'd sneak out over my backyard on to the wall of Mr Cartwright's stables. The windows would be shoved up and I'd hear the sleepy voices and see their white faces. Mainly Mr Jackson, because he was always very nervous and afraid the police would be coming after him because he was in jail once for robbing lead off people's houses, and we weren't allowed play with them. That time when I became a Protestant and was going with Hattie Hobson she'd arrange a time and open her curtains when she was getting ready for bed. When she'd take off her vest I could see everything with my big torch but her bosoms were tiny and nothing like as big as Nurse Bannister's. I think that's why Tommy got fed up with Hattie Hobson. Everything was very still on the veranda so I opened my eyes.

It seemed much emptier now without Derek. I missed his questions, his laugh, his jokes. The week after he died another boy was able to go home. He was only in for physio for his club foot and said his ma missed him and had got him signed out. I wished my ma would do the same. But at least I still had Nurse Feeney. After the kiss I felt much older and had grown ten new hairs and even Da said I was getting a bit taller. But I wasn't getting much sleep because after what happened with Derek I didn't want to take any more chances and I stayed awake until a quarter past two when the night nurses were having their tea break and I'd go around all my pals and put my hand on their foreheads and say the prayer. Nurse Feeney and me kissed nearly every night now so I didn't really mind staying awake and thinking of home. And I think Nurse Bannister was jealous because I was the only boy in the hospital with pubic hair that wouldn't feel her diddies. I was in the bathroom with the huge mirror one day, counting them, when Nurse Bannister came in and caught me. She blackmailed me and said she'd tell everyone unless I rubbed her diddies from the inside so I did.

It was the worst sin I'd ever committed – a big black mortaller! If only the deaf priest from Finglas was working in here. But no – just a very young one with Brylcreem in his hair, that had probably never even heard the word diddies. I put off confession and going to communion for two whole weeks, but I was nearly vomiting with guilt, so I had to tell him. There was no confession boxes in the hospital. The priest used Matron's office and all the lads swore she used to listen outside. So I whispered it so low he asked was I in for laryngitis. When he finally heard the terrible thing I did, I knew by his face it was very serious. It was probably a sin you had to bring to the Archbishop when he was sober. He said nothing for ages. Then he just smiled and gave me absolution and just three Hail Marys as penance. I wanted to hug him I was so happy. Then I made the mistake of blabbing on about maybe I might become a priest and about me having been in the Third Order of St Francis, but at least I said nothing about throwing the brown habit into the canal and I never said a word to him about Nurse Feeney.

Nurse Feeney couldn't have been watching my terrible sin with Nurse Bannister but somehow she knew. After we kissed that night she pushed me away and didn't speak to me for three whole days. I swore to myself then and there that I'd never do it again. Even Da that Sunday left in under an hour and I wondered if I had the mark of Cain on my forehead even though I hadn't murdered anyone. Ma said he wasn't feeling that great, and it was probably his pleurisy. I didn't really believe her but at least she didn't notice anything different about me and even said the doctors told her I'd be home for Christmas. It was one of those winter Sundays where there was loads of visitors to see me in their wet gabardine coats so I didn't tell her about my plan to marry Nurse Feeney.

The two empty beds were soon filled. Michael Porter was back, cured from the scarlet fever. He was on crutches with the whole top of his body covered in plaster of Paris including his head. You could barely see his face but he had twinkling eyes and I liked him a lot.

I hated the other new boy, Peter Fitzgerald. I hated

everything about him. Same age as me but bigger and the worst thing, all the nurses said he had lovely brown eyes. He was put in the other empty bed – Derek's – my dead best pal. He was only in for round shoulders and thought he could run as fast and as long as me. Everyone loved him and said he was really funny but I could see through him straight away.

Auntie Bridie came to tell me the bad news. It was Wednesday the eleventh of November. It had been a lovely sunny day and I'd been racing Peter Fitzgerald about a hundred laps around the playground. I was easily eight laps ahead but he wouldn't give up. He was like that. He was trying to show off in front of Nurse Feeney and he kept cheating and cutting corners, but I didn't care because I'd had loads of practice. When I saw Nurse Feeney coming towards us I speeded up as fast as I could go.

'Robbie, you have a visitor.' I knew by the look on her face she was back in love with me again.

The visitors' room was in the main house and Auntie Bridie was smoking a cigarette. I'd forgotten how much I liked her. When her husband, my Uncle Phil, got TB their whole family came to stay with us for nearly two years and she'd always persuade Ma to let us play out on the street much later than usual.

'Your da's in hospital getting an operation.' She handed me the big packet of crisps and sweets and apples. Even though she talked to me for over half an hour that was the only thing I heard her say. They'd been telling me lies about the pleurisy. It was cancer of the stomach. Afterwards Peter Fitzgerald told me that Nurse Bannister said there was no cure for that and my da was going to die. I knew I had to get to him fast. I knew I could cure him. But I had to get to see him.

Sister Conroy did her best but the Matron said under no circumstances. Nobody had ever escaped from the hospital. Richard Mooney told me the last time two of them tried they were caught in less than an hour. The stupid grey uniforms were a giveaway. They hadn't taken Peter Fitzgerald's street clothes away from him and he was only a bit bigger than me but he wouldn't give me a lend. Nurse Feeney said I was mad and I'd get into big trouble, but she told me where the Mater Hospital was and to be careful, and Richard Mooney lent me two bob. You'd think Peter Fitzgerald knew what I was up to because he didn't go asleep for ages. Michael Porter had extra pillows because he had to sleep sitting up but he lent them to me and helped me stuff up my bed. I hated wearing Peter Fitzgerald's clothes but at least there was a penknife in one of the pockets. Thank God it was a bank holiday – no sisters or nurses around.

It didn't take me long to cross the back garden and get out onto the road, and I didn't think Peter Fitzgerald would ever notice the rip in his trousers from the barbed wire. The bus conductor looked at me a bit funny but he gave me the change from the two bob and never said a word. I ran all the way up the North Circular Road. Thank God I'd been practising and it didn't take long. The man at the desk said visiting time was over and he wouldn't tell me the ward. Then the head thing happened to me again and I knew it was St John's Ward.

'Did you hear me, son? Visiting time's over. Now leave.' But I knew my way around the Mater Hospital since when I was there after Patrick's Day, so I slammed the door to annoy him and ran down around the lane. That's where they always have the casualty place. A woman that looked like Ma was walking down the lane with her head down, crying. But it couldn't have been her because she looked so old. Once she passed I bent down and used the penknife to make my knee bleed and then I limped in to the nurse. I needn't have bothered. There was a huge queue and nobody noticed me going down the corridor on my way to the wards. Da's bed was just inside the door. There were loads of tubes coming out of him and I felt like crying but I couldn't. He was definitely still unconscious because when I put my cold hand on his head he never moved.

The man in the bed beside him asked me if I was Robbie because he'd heard him mumbling my name. He told me I'd just missed my ma, but Da was asleep when she came in so she left the parcel in his locker before she left. He said she'd been talking to one of the nurses outside in the corridor for ages and then came back in to kiss him goodbye, and if I ran fast I'd catch her.

She must have thought he was going to die. I thought I saw a smile on Da's face, but I took my two hands off his forehead and left before the man could ask what I was doing. But I knew for certain that Da wasn't going to die. Outside on the street I became really excited. There were loads of cars and people everywhere. I couldn't help it. I went in to a chipper and bought two bags of chips and ate them walking back down the North Circular Road. It was the first real food I'd had in months.

I stopped for ages at the Five Lamps and looked down under the arches. I was only five minutes from my house. I was dying to go and tell them that Da was cured, and I really missed my baby sister Mary Joe. I even saw a dog that looked like Bobby but when I caught up with him it wasn't. Anyway if I got back without being noticed, I could always escape again. I started walking down the North Strand towards Fairview Park. I was leaning on the bridge looking over at the trains shunting, where me and Da always went for a walk. That's when I changed my mind. There was a man coming out of Cusack's pub wearing the same cap as my da. He was a bit drunk but

I knew he wouldn't mind. I was beginning to like Peter Fitzgerald a bit now because there was a little pencil and paper in one of the pockets. I asked the drunk man to write the note. It took a few goes but he finally got it right and never asked me why.

'Jimmy is OK. He's not going to die.' That way they'd never know it was me. My heart was thumping all the way up Emerald Street but I couldn't stop to think. There was no lights on in the house and I slipped it in the letter box and I was gone in a flash because Bobby started barking like mad. That was the fastest I ever ran back out through Fairview Park. I didn't even chance the buses again. I had to wait for a while outside the hospital to get my breath back. Everything was back in place now and it had been easy to sneak back in. I was definitely going to do it again. But my heart wouldn't stop thumping for ages and my knee was really sore.

I lay on the bed that night thinking of the brass letter box on the door and the shunting train and the new name over Darcy's shop. I could still smell the new tar on Emerald Street and the chips but most of all I remembered Da's sick face. I just had to get out. Maybe get a doctor to discharge me – the only way. The next day Sister Conroy agreed with a smile but the doctor she got me was very old and smelt of whiskey. In Matron's office, he got me to take off all my clothes. Matron was watching as he walked around me doing his doctor's stuff but I didn't care.

'Nothing wrong there. Everything right with the heart. No fevers, no diseases. Walk backwards and forwards. Ah that's it, you've got very flat feet, must build up the arches. And the shoulders, a bit stooped. Some time in the gym will do you no harm.' He never even mentioned the head thing.

'Put your clothes back on.' He was sitting at the desk writing in a thick file. 'Three months in the gym or you'll have a hump.' He was looking at the cover of the file. 'Peter Fitzgerald – a good Cavan name.'

'I'm not Peter Fitzgerald! There's fuck all wrong with me!' I couldn't help it. 'Check my head! Check my fucking head!'

The doddery oul bollix had mixed up my name. They put me down for flat feet and round shoulders, and no matter how many times I told them they wouldn't believe me. At least the gym was brilliant and had loads of stuff – trapezes and exercise bars and ropes with rings like a circus and even a trampoline. And the nurses weren't really nurses – physio staff – much older in crisp white uniforms, make-up and long nails they'd spend the whole time painting red.

They only showed you once what to do and left you at it. I was so determined to fix the flat feet fast that I spent all day bar dinner time in there and I was always the last one out. I'd decided it would take about a week; I'd easily be home for Christmas. You had to pick up pencils with your toes and walk along a wooden beam, but the ropes and the pull-up bars were more fun and even though I didn't have round shoulders I spent most of my time on them. Anyway I had very strong arms from Bobby pulling me so they were easy. Peter Fitzgerald was really stupid because he skipped his exercises nearly always and I even warned him he'd be in there forever.

The next Sunday Ma was in first. She told me Da was on the mend. She leaned in close and said Granny Wilson told her she'd seen my ghost at midnight during the week, and she handed me the note. She'd been called in to see my new doddery oul doctor and told him about my head accident. I read it slowly and could feel my toes tingle.

Then the sun burst through the clouds and the whole veranda lit up, and Ma's face looked so young.

It was a perfect moment. Richard Mooney was in his wheelchair laughing as Michael Porter with his twinkly eyes and without his crutches pushed him around the playground. Nurse Feeney was going off duty somewhere in her white blouse and her short blue skirt. Tommy Lyons with his hair sleeked back was getting orange juice for the whole ward. Sister Conroy was smiling and swaying in her office as she listened to the radio playing a beautiful song called 'Twenty-four Hours From Tulsa'. Maybe it wouldn't be long before I saw Da.

Everything changed completely. They gave me an isolation room on my own but still on the veranda. Everyone spoke to me different and I could have visitors on Wednesday afternoons as well. I could have as many books from the library as I wanted, and even the food was better. Ma must have said something to them about my head accident, because they were almost afraid of me – except Nurse Feeney. Peter Fitzgerald wasn't as stupid as I thought. Instead of going to the gym every day to fix himself he was chatting up Nurse Feeney. I didn't even know that she'd moved to day duty and was falling in love with him and had betrayed me. Richard Mooney told me about it. He was still my best pal. She used to visit me every day but I refused to speak to her even though I wanted to and one day she started crying and told me she was going to go back down to a hospital in the country, if we couldn't be friends.

Suddenly Nurse Bannister wanted to be my best pal. When she was on night duty she'd come into my room. She had a boyfriend who was mad into horses and she'd let me pick the winner from the paper. I was hardly ever wrong and she wanted me to touch her breasts from the inside. I'd promised God I'd never do that again, but when I got the Grand National right she came in with a bottle of wine. She must have drunk a lot of it because she gave me a sip and I wanted to go asleep straight away but she got into bed beside me and wanted me to give one of her huge bosoms a kiss. When I woke up she was kissing my lips and then started down there. I told her to stop because I still loved Nurse Feeney. All the wine and that stuff was making my head burst and I wanted to get back on the veranda with my pals and I still hadn't seen my da. Nurse Bannister must have been afraid I'd say something, or maybe because I wanted it so much, but I was soon back in my old bed looking out at the stars.

Most of the boys were getting ready to be sent home for Christmas. Even the bedridden ones with crutches were packing their bags. I had mine packed and ready for days. Sister Conroy had a man in painting holly and ivy and Santa's sleigh on the windows and I knew that some of them were not going home. But I made a vow to myself to come back in and visit whoever was left. I bought a present for Nurse Feeney and prayed to God she'd be on duty on Christmas Day when I came back to visit.

It was a lovely nearly a hundred carat gold ring that I'd been saving up for months to buy her. One of the really nice posh nurses from the gym, who listened to all my secrets and never let me down, had bought it at a great price for me because her boyfriend was a jeweller man in Weir's in Grafton Street, and she'd kept the receipt for me in case it wasn't the right size. But that Halloween in the hospital when I got the ring in my piece of barmbrack, Nurse Feeney tried it on so I knew it would be perfect.

Nurse Feeney was the one person I'd miss the most when I got home. I couldn't even bear one day without seeing her and I knew that the minute I gave her the new gold ring she'd forget about Peter Fitzgerald and marry me, even though I would miss Richard Mooney and Michael Porter and my best friend Jim Clancy, but at least they'd be going home for Christmas as well.

The night before Christmas Eve everyone was so excited, even the few boys who couldn't be let out because they needed constant attention. Even though I knew there was no such thing as Santy, we all had to write a letter, but at least I could put my own magical address. Da's present was the last thing I packed that night but not the last thing I did. I didn't want to tell my pals I was going home forever, so I waited until they were all asleep, and wrote them all a letter, promising I would never forget them and always come and visit every Sunday. I'd make sure nobody ever, ever lost their files and somehow do something about the horrible food.

I lay in bed that night thinking that Da, if he was well enough, would be fixing up the Christmas-tree lights and maybe Ma and Theresa would have a glass of sherry. I got a lovely present for Bobby, a collar with our Emerald Street address, in case Clicky Kelly's gang ever kidnapped him. I knew this was the one Christmas I'd get Uncle Mick to come in to the parlour on Christmas night and play games with us and not stay on his own. I made a promise to God that I'd go out to Glasnevin Cemetery with him on Stephen's Day, and help him trim the little hedge that was cut into the shape of a crucifix around Ellen's grave, even though I'd want to play with my toys, because I didn't want him to be lonely at Christmas any more.

It was Sister Conroy who broke the bad news. She wasn't even on night duty but she wanted to tell me herself. I was still awake because I'd just finished putting my farewell letters under all my sleeping pals' pillows. That poor doddery old bollix, my new doctor, had died of a heart attack that very morning, probably from the whiskey. There was nobody left that could sign my release, and I wasn't going home.

It was Christmas Day and I got loads of visitors. The Vincent de Paul were first in and I got a xylophone. The Legion of Mary man was next with one arm as long as another. They were only allowed give spiritual aid so I couldn't play with the xylophone until he'd finished telling me the true story of Christmas. Then an old man loaded with parcels staggered towards me.

Even Da had been let out for Christmas but I hardly recognised him as he stood by my bed. Shea had warned me that he'd lost a lot of weight – but I wasn't ready for this. His smile seemed bigger than ever but his face looked small. I pretended not to notice and gave him a big hug and his present, a new pipe from Kapp and Peterson's, and an ounce of tin twist plug tobacco. It cost five shillings but I'd been saving hard and spent most of it on him. I'm glad Nurse Feeney was off duty till later because he didn't look like Clark Gable any more. Funny, the longer he sat there the younger he looked.

They must have all come in the same bus. Everyone was there, Ma, Tommy, Shea, Elaine and Mary Joe in guess what – a nurse's uniform from Santa – Auntie Chrissie and Bridie and loads of my cousins with presents, and there was so many empty beds they could all pull up a seat, and sure enough as I opened my present I knew what it was – another huge xylophone. Da wanted to be last to leave but Tommy stayed with him to help him out. Da pulled my present from his big black coat pocket and told me not to open it till later. Tommy winked at him and they both took a slug out of a baby Powers bottle before they left. The one hope in my heart was that I'd get to see Nurse Feeney.

Those of us left in the hospital that could walk were allowed into the nurses' Christmas party in the gym. Nurse Bannister was very drunk and I avoided her like the plague. Even Matron was tipsy and asked me up to dance. Elaine had taught me to jive but Matron was far too heavy to swing around like that. It was very crowded but I could see the back of a girl in the corner with long black hair and a red dancing dress. When she turned it was Nurse Feeney and she was holding a proper boyfriend's hand. He looked too old for her and I didn't want her to see me. But they must have, because when I was running out I heard him laughing and I'd say it was about me.

Every bed on the veranda was empty. You could still hear the music from the party. All the presents from the Vincent de Paul were left on their lockers for the boys who'd been brought home. I swapped my xylophone for Richard Mooney's cavalry soldiers. I knew he wouldn't mind. I sat on my bed and hoped Da was enjoying the pipe. I took Nurse Feeney's name off her present and got into bed in my clothes. Way in the distance I could hear them all still singing. It was 'Silent Night'.

Da looked much better the next Sunday and didn't need anyone to help him walk. They were nearly all there again because it was New Year's Day. They'd brought a present from Uncle Paul, our rich uncle. They were dying for me to open it. It was a big heavy square parcel wrapped in brown paper. Elaine said she'd bet her new boyfriend Joe it was a tape recorder. Tommy said no, it was bound to be a record player and he'd mind it for me till I got home. I ripped the paper off. There was loads of wrapping. A tin box of Goldgrain biscuits! Not

even chocolate! It was the first time I cursed in front of
my ma.

I still hadn't opened Da's present. It was wrapped in brown
paper with string. He'd written on it, 'To Robbie – Love
Da' and three x's. It was nearly six inches long and rectan-
gular, but no matter how I shook it I couldn't hear a
thing. At least it wasn't a xylophone. I made a vow that
I'd never open it until I was out of this kip of a hospital
for good. Even though I was often tempted, at least I
kept that vow. Somehow I realised that maybe God hadn't
wanted me to leave the hospital that Christmas because
I had more jobs to do, so I gave up being grumpy. I even
forgave Nurse Feeney for getting a proper boyfriend. At
least she seemed to have given up Peter Fitzgerald and
he was going mad. She was being so nice to me again I
forgave her for everything, but I didn't give her the ring
yet, maybe on her birthday, but we were definitely back
being good friends. With all the excitement of nearly
getting home for Christmas I'd almost forgotten about
my picture of Jesus and my promise to God so maybe
that's why all the bad things happened to me. I couldn't
wait to do my next miracle and it didn't take long.
  One night me and Nurse Feeney were having our usual
little chat. She was sitting on the side of my bed. I couldn't
believe it when she told me she had to go to London for
an operation, and wouldn't be coming back, and that she'd
never talk to her boyfriend again, but that she'd always
love me. She started crying when I told her the secret
about me being able to fix everything if you weren't well
and she said I was too young to understand. Little did
she know. When she went up to the night-nurses' office
I put my picture of Jesus under the pillow.
  I must have fallen asleep really fast because it was nearly
bright outside and the wind had died down and there

was Nurse Feeney and Nurse Bannister shouting and laughing at the end of the bed. They were hugging each other and Nurse Feeney said I must be a little genius but she had to go home now because she had terrible cramps in her stomach, but she wouldn't have to go to London now or leave the hospital and I said I could fix her cramps too. They left smiling and that was when I decided that I'd marry Nurse Feeney and could still do miracles without having to become a priest. I put the picture of Jesus back in the locker under the cards and the crisps and went to help the day nurses with the bedpans and the breakfast.

Jim Clancy was brilliant at table tennis. He didn't need his crutches either because he'd steady himself with one hand on the table. He could reach all the shots with his other hand, except when he had to serve. He'd have to throw the ball up with his other hand and if you hit it back into the far corner, he'd nearly fall over, but I'd never do that. His girlfriend was in for bad leg muscles. She had red curly hair and freckles and Jim Clancy was mad about her and loved to kiss her.

He was always very faithful to her and never went near Nurse Bannister. Our teacher, Mrs Grant, was really old, nearly sixty, and said she came from the same place as my ma in the country in County Wexford so she was always nice to me, and she liked Jim Clancy too, even when he didn't get his sums right, because he was such a gentleman, and didn't hide the chalk on her like the other older boys. She never knew he couldn't read because I'd teach him to learn the page off by heart. She said she remembered when Ma was a young beautiful girl with red hair just like Jim Clancy's girlfriend, and I never knew that.

One day she brought in forms for the Texaco painting competition and we all decided to have a go. I drew a

picture of the sun setting behind two big Kerry mountains with loads of sheep on one side and a big white
horse high up on the hill on the other, just like the place
I was going to buy in Howth for me and Da and all of
us. But Tommy Lyons said I was a stupid bollix because
the sun always went down in Galway and had I never
heard the song. So I tore it up and started again. This
time I played safe with the sun high in the sky and one
big white house in Howth looking over the sea with loads
of yachts with red sails.

Jim Clancy was brilliant at drawing. He could even
make up his own birthday cards for kids in the ward and
did a brilliant valentine for his girlfriend. The picture he
drew for the competition was of his church in
Castledermot and a graveyard with a huge tombstone
with his da's name and R.I.P. and 'Gone Fishing' 'cos
that's what his ma would always tell him whenever he
asked her what had happened. Richard Mooney's one
was mad with a huge dagger going through the roof of
a big mansion that looked like our hospital with splashes
of colour all around. I thought it was the best and would
definitely win.

About three weeks later, when we were having our
bread and jam at teatime, Matron came in all smiles and
said that me and Jim Clancy had won a prize and a car
would be coming for us next week to take us to the ball-
room in the Hibernian Hotel where we'd be collecting
them and that there'd be loads of photographs, and we
might be on the radio. I was delighted, but couldn't believe
Richard Mooney hadn't won, especially as he painted with
his feet. He didn't seem to mind though and I was glad
Tommy Lyons didn't tell him what he heard Sister Conroy
say to one of the nurses later that night, that it was a
shame Matron wouldn't let them send his picture in. They
got us a loan of two suits, two white shirts and two red

ties and we couldn't wait for the big night. We were left waiting in the visitors' room in the hospital that night for ages and all the nurses kept sneaking in to see how well we looked. When the car came we were both shaking with nerves because we might be talking on the wireless and the whole hospital was being allowed to stay up and listen just in case. Matron had written out a speech for both of us. When she left, Jim Clancy tore up his one and whispered to me that he had his own one ready and there was feck all they could do about that!

Outside the hotel there was huge crowds of people arriving from everywhere, and they had two wheelchairs ready for us. I winked at Jim Clancy and begged him not to say anything 'cos I'd never get a chance like this again and the girl pushing my wheelchair was really beautiful. I couldn't believe how kind everyone was to us and we were pushed up on the stage with about twenty other boys and girls in the whole of their health. We were put up the front and I felt very bad about cheating in the wheelchair but it was too late to do anything about it now and I started sweating when all the photographers started flashing away.

There was a man called Harry Thullier who was very famous presenting the prizes and he got all the audience to do a three-two-one countdown before we went on the air. He gave out all the big prizes first, and all the kids had been warned to say how brilliant Texaco was. Then it was our turn. I was shoved over first and was really nervous, but I read out Matron's speech and got a huge clap. Then it was Jim Clancy's turn and he was grinning and wasn't nervous at all. There was dead silence when he started talking about how terrible the hospital was and the horrible food and how you were only allowed visitors once a week, and if Texaco were any good at all they'd get the government to sort the kip out.

Thank God Mr Harry Thullier was really good at his job and had copped on straight away what was going on. So he cut off Jim Clancy's microphone and had music playing, so neither of us got into trouble when we got back. Except on the way out I saw a kid from my Christian Brothers school in the distance and jumped out of the wheelchair to run after him. Some of the audience people near me started booing at me and I was glad when that night was over. But at least we had two huge boxes of chocolates to share with our pals and two cards each that would allow us buy things in Brown Thomas for a guinea each.

The physio nurses in the gym were very annoyed when they heard Richard Mooney's painting wasn't even allowed to be sent in to the competition. On the week before Valentine's Day they brought him into the gym even though he couldn't swing on the bars or anything, and got him to paint special cards for their boyfriends and write puzzles and rude rhymes. They made a big fuss over him and they all gave him money. Outside of Nurse Feeney, I liked them the best in the whole hospital. They were the only ones that went in for St Patrick's Day. They brought in bunches of shamrock for everyone and painted all the girls' toenails green, even those in wheelchairs. It wasn't Sunday so there was no visitors. Nurse Conroy said she'd let me listen to the match in her office because she knew I'd nearly died on St Patrick's Day. I wondered were Shea and my gang up in Croker. I thought of the picture with the smiling eyes and I knew Jesus was happy with me and didn't mind about my few sins.

The next week Jim Clancy had a great idea. He'd read a crime book out of the library and said you could easily hire a private detective to find his da. So he got the posh nurses in the gym to buy the Brown Thomas vouchers off us to buy nail varnish and stuff. I didn't mind at all because once the detective found him, he'd get out and get a job as a worker in a sweet shop and pay me back straight away.

There was no address for Hercule Poirot in the Agatha Christie books, so we had to come up with another plan. I sat down with him one night and tried to get all the information from him about his da, but it was useless, he could hardly remember anything. But then I had a great idea and he let me hypnotise him, and then it all came out. He began to remember things − slowly at first but then it came out so fast I nearly ran out of paper and had to rob some from the night-nurses' office when they ran over there after we told them that we'd heard someone in the girls' ward screaming they were having a heart attack and a fit. I filled nearly four pages and it took me ages to wake him up.

His ma was right − Jim's da had gone away on a big ship from Galway bringing turf to India and never came back. He remembered he'd got a Christmas card from Calcutta with three elephants, and that was the last one he ever got so he must still be there. There was loads of people on the elephants and palm trees and not even a drop of snow. Next day when we looked up the atlas in the library India was only four fingers away, except you have to go on a ship to get there. Then I got another brilliant idea. Mr Brown, the man from our street that drove the ships, was still my best friend if he hadn't died yet and Jim Clancy was really excited when I told him about the night he nearly brought me to Brazil only for I'd forgotten to leave a note for my younger sister Mary Joe.

The next Sunday, at visiting time, I started asking Ma about all the neighbours and thank God Mr Brown was still alive. When I told her I'd love to see him and could she get him to come in to visit she was very suspicious at first. But when I told her I wanted to apologise to him for nearly getting him into trouble over my trip to Brazil, she laughed and said she'd do her best, although he was very busy because his eldest daughter Elizabeth was getting married.

The minute she left I told Jim Clancy we needed another plan. Luckily it was very sunny for the next two weeks and we lay out in it from eight in the morning until it got dark, because we didn't want to look suspicious like milk bottles when we got to India. My older sister Elaine had told me a great trick so I stole some baby oil from the babies' ward but it was very greasy and you had to scrub it off every night and it had a terrible sweet smell, and we still hadn't figured out how we'd get some of the nurses to give us a smallpox injection because we'd read about that in a travel book from the library about Indonesia which wasn't that far away from Calcutta where his da had gone fishing. Then an amazing thing happened for Jim Clancy though it left me a little bit sad.

The baby oil was working – specially on him – and he looked so dark and handsome all the nurses were beginning to fancy him, but he'd already promised his girlfriend with the red hair that once his da got back, he'd get out and pay me back the money and marry her, so he'd never mess with them, no matter how hard they tried, especially Nurse Bannister. His ma only could visit him once every month and even though she didn't have much money she'd always bring him up loads of sweets and presents that he'd share with all of us. They would all be gone in three days but that was all right because me and Michael Porter and Richard Mooney would make sure that he'd have anything he wanted from our parcels, even money, if he swore he wouldn't play poker.

Anyway, that Sunday, just before we were going to escape to India to find his da, his ma came in with a man in a suit. He must have been a millionaire because he gave us each five bob, everyone on the veranda, even the girls' ward, and he had two brown leather suitcases and he was holding Jim Clancy's mother's hand and she was laughing all the time and told him to pack his clothes and stuff. The man even looked like a doctor and maybe that's why Matron was really nice to him but it all happened too fast, I just had time to whisper to him that I'd mind his girlfriend for him and then suddenly Jim Clancy was gone forever.

Mary Rigney cried for three and a half days and nearly washed away all her freckles. Maybe Jim Clancy didn't have time to say a proper goodbye. I heard the nurses from the girls' ward talking about her. That was the first time I knew her real name. Jim Clancy always used call her 'Princess' and didn't care who jeered him about that. The nurses said she'd given up eating but nobody could blame her for that.

They never let you visit the girls' ward unless you were doing a message for one of the nurses, but when I asked they said it would be OK for a short while but I'd have to leave if there was any bedpan stuff going on. I hoped she wouldn't go hysterical so I brought my picture of Jesus folded into my pocket just in case.

Most of them in the girls' ward were bedridden ones, although Mary Rigney was allowed up for a few hours every day. At first she didn't like me at all and told me no matter what I said I wouldn't get a kiss off her. I told her a big lie that Jim Clancy had asked me to teach her the harmonica so that when she got out to get married to him and live over their sweet shop she could play lullabies to all their babies. That worked brilliant and she could play the whole scales up and down after our first lesson. She said she had a good ear for music and they had a big piano at home with only high notes missing, and even though her da was a police sergeant in Portlaoise he could play anything at all with his two hands. Thank God she wasn't from Meath.

None of us had got the address of Jim Clancy's house but I remembered it was Castledermot and I promised I'd bring over the atlas map the next day and measure how far his house was from Portlaoise where Mary Rigney lived.

The girl in the next bed was a tinker with poliomyelitis and she had lovely black hair and a suntan better than Jim Clancy or me, and it was great because she knew loads of lullabies and swore she'd teach them to Mary Rigney for all her babies. Her name was Monica Maughan and she got tons of visitors every Sunday and they'd have to be let in in groups of six. She got more parcels than nearly everyone else put together and she lived in Galway and Skerries and Cork. She was bedridden at the moment but her da and her brothers had made their own wheel-chair for her for when she got out and used to practise every Sunday, whizzing her up and down the veranda, and give all the other girls a go. Her da was huge and used to be a boxer for Ireland and could lift any of the girls from the bed with one arm and Monica Maughan was Mary Rigney's best friend.

I couldn't call Mary Rigney Princess, that wouldn't have been fair, but I asked her could I call her Tinkerbell and she said that was OK, but I'd still never get a kiss off her even though we could be friends. When Jim Clancy left, even though he was quiet enough, you really missed him, and it was raining outside so there was nothing to do. I didn't even thump Peter Fitzgerald when he jeered me about my new friend Tinkerbell, but at least she'd stopped crying. So I lay on the bed. The hospital requests programme was on the wireless and they were all stupid songs. Then the man read out a special request to 'Princess from her Castledermot boyfriend' and they played 'Roses are Red', but you couldn't hear the words with all the cheering from the girls' ward and we all joined in. Even the nurses were running around laughing and excited, so I took my picture out of my pocket and looked at it for a long time. Then I put it carefully back in my locker under all my stuff and hoped Tinkerbell would still be my friend and I could still go over there because there was an awful lot of girls to cure and some of them looked very sick to me.

Something magical must have happened that day and it must have been Jim Clancy's song because from then on we were allowed go over to visit the girls' ward, between a quarter past two and three except on Sundays, and they were allowed come over to us, and at last Richard Mooney got a girlfriend and so did nearly everyone else. Michael Porter was giving out hell. He said we shouldn't be rushing into things and to play hard to get. I don't think he liked girls that much. But it was only for three-quarters of an hour every day and even the bedridden ones and the orphans were getting visitors.

Tommy Lyons and the two older boys with pubic hair were getting on great with some of the older girls and I think Nurse Bannister was raging. Richard Mooney's new girlfriend was Carmel Tucker. She was a Protestant from Wicklow, but that didn't matter 'cos they were only starting to go out and they owned a huge house. She had a club foot but could walk a good bit and she was mad about him. They'd play cards and snakes and ladders and he must have liked her a lot because he'd always let her win. She said she was in for a short while and that worried Richard Mooney until I promised him I'd steal and hide her file.

Michael Porter pretended he couldn't care less and he'd walk with his crutches in the playground on his own, muttering and cursing to himself until all the dating was over and everyone was back in their own ward. What changed his mind about the whole thing was when Nurse Bannister tried to get him into the toilet on their own and he decided to get a girl for himself. But nearly everyone was hitched up now except Monica Maughan so he decided to give her a go.

I went with him the first time but she told him to feck off – she'd never marry a cripple. That didn't bother him at all. I think he liked a challenge and he'd go over there every day and sit beside her bed even though she wouldn't speak to him, not even one word. Then he had a brain-wave. He told her his name was really Michael Ward, and they lived in a caravan near Liverpool. That worked brilliant for a while and they were getting on great until the first visiting Sunday after she swore she'd marry him. All the Maughan family rushed in to him and slapped him on the back and asked him loads of questions. He was a great liar and got away with it, but Mr Maughan lifted him into the wheelchair and her brothers ran up and down the wards with him and her da before he left warned him not to lay a finger on her till they were wed or he'd kill him. Then he laughed and shook Michael Porter's hand and nearly broke it and gave him a ten-shilling note.

When they all left Michael Porter came over to me and swore he'd kill me for starting the whole thing off and how in the name of Jaysus was he going to get out of this. I knew he was upset because he hardly ever cursed, and he was really shaking.

Peter Fitzgerald spoiled the whole thing. His girlfriend was Sarah Ryder and wasn't a cripple. I didn't think she was one bit pretty but everyone said she had very well-developed bosoms for her age and she certainly had. Michael Porter noticed it first and told me they used to sneak off during the visiting and they were up to no good. I saw them sneaking into the storeroom for the bedpans one day and that's where they were caught. He said they were only practising doctors and nurses, but Sister Conroy was furious and called the whole visiting thing off after only two weeks. She said Matron was back from her holidays that weekend and probably wouldn't have agreed to it anyway.

I think Michael Porter must have squealed on them because everyone in the whole hospital was raging except him and Nurse Bannister. But, for whatever reason, I was still allowed visit my friend Tinkerbell anytime I wanted and could sneak messages over for all of them and back real easy. Richard Mooney used to write pages and pages of poems and stuff with his foot for Carmel Tucker, and even some paintings and you'd nearly need a suitcase just for his stuff alone, although Michael Porter came out of the trouble very well because he didn't ever write anything to Monica Maughan again but her da would still drop him the ten-shilling note every Sunday.

The weather was getting better now and we were back playing outside and everything was back to normal. There was no word from Jim Clancy and nobody seemed to miss him, even Tinkerbell, who hardly ever mentioned his name and I certainly wasn't going to, because I was getting to like her a lot, and I hadn't kissed her once so I didn't let him down. She was getting stronger now and once or twice when she was helping me feed the rabbits she'd come behind me and jump up on my back and ask for a jockey ride, and that's as far as it went except she begged me to meet her da.

I was a bit afraid of policemen since that morning in

11 Emerald Street when my older brother Tommy was nearly arrested for having borrowed a stolen little transistor radio from Michael Carney in the flats. Michael Carney used to call around nearly every day to lend Tommy things, but it always reminded me of the comics I used to lend to Marian Casey's brother, and I knew he fancied Elaine, and that he was up to no good. OK, he had long locks, but he didn't look a bit like Elvis, and anyway Elaine was going out with Joe Connolly so he had no chance. But when the police came around early that morning, they frightened the life out of Ma and Da and I knew Tommy was in big trouble so I set Bobby my dog on them and pretended it was a mistake. They left very fast. I was Tommy's big hero after that for nearly a week, even though he was in loads of trouble at home, and he never forgot that and said I could have Hattie Hobson back if I wanted, and that he was going to go straight from now on, and never let Ma and Da down again and – as far as I can remember – he never did.

But Tinkerbell's da was a lovely man, not like a policeman at all, and hardly ever wore his uniform when he came in to visit. Him and Da became great friends one day when he sorted out some summons Da got for driving on the wrong side of the footpath and every Sunday after that Da would bring in a lovely big Granny Smith apple for Tinkerbell and even shake hands with all of Monica Maughan's family, and he was the only one to do that. Once I was really delighted to see Mr Maughan wince when Da shook his hand, even though Da was still sick then. I knew that when I grew up I'd have the same strong handshake as Da and that was the Sunday I made Da promise that he'd bring my dog Bobby in to see me.

The very next Sunday it was like I'd never been away from him. Bobby ran straight in the gate and jumped on my bed and started licking me. Da had had to walk all the way up even though he was still very skinny from the cancer thing, because all the conductors remembered Bobby from the Dollymount trips, and wouldn't let them on. He was the one person I really wanted to see and it was nearly my best Sunday ever in there until what happened later. He sat on my bed and wouldn't stop licking me until Da followed. Then I did a foolish thing. I brought him on the lead for a walk around the boys' ward. He loved Michael Porter the best and wouldn't leave his side until I dragged him over to the girls' ward to meet my new friend Tinkerbell. I'd told her so much about Bobby she was delighted to see him, and he even seemed to like her. But it was one of the few times when her da came in wearing his uniform. Bobby went berserk, barking and snapping at his heels. He was really a nice man and he did his best to be friends, holding out biscuits, but Bobby hated uniforms and when Sergeant Rigney had to make a swipe at him with his big black shoe I let the lead go and he just ran straight out across the play-ground and disappeared into the bushes.

I ran as fast as I could because I knew exactly where he was heading and I'd seen him chase the hares in Dollymount. The rabbits were terrified, all scrunched up in a corner, but luckily they'd made the hutch wires really strong and he couldn't get in. He was bigger now than I'd remembered, but so was I and I managed to drag him outside the visitors' gate and called out to Da to follow me quick. As I watched him pull Da down the avenue past the bus stop, I knew Da would never do this again. But Mr Rigney was nice to me when I went back in to apologise and said my da was a lovely man.

That was the day Michael Porter decided he'd get a dog of his own. He said he was fed up with girls, they were too much trouble. He wanted to get a big dog, a St Bernard or an Irish wolfhound. Richard Mooney's girlfriend

Carmel Tucker knew all about dogs because they had kennels in their huge mansion in Wicklow. She said they were all thoroughbreds or something and would cost a fortune, but Michael Porter was still getting his ten shillings every Sunday from Monica Maughan's da and was really rich so that wasn't a problem.

They'd got us the rabbits, but nobody really owned them and you couldn't even chase them unless you were in the whole of your health and that wouldn't work for Michael Porter, so he woke up the next morning and said a cat would be grand, they did their own thing and even killed off mice so there was no way Matron would say no. If she did, he would kill himself anyway because he was fed up with the whole kip of a hospital and needed a pet just for himself. I decided not to ask Da for help because he had enough trouble of his own.

There were loads of cats in the city, but out here in the country in Clontarf, do you think we could find one? Me and Peter Fitzgerald were having a truce at the time and we went out on a scouting mission every night for a week, in every back garden we could find. We cornered a big smelly tomcat one night, but it nearly scratched our faces off when we tried to catch it, and anyway it could never be tamed into a pet for Michael Porter so that was no use. And the oul fella in the house nearly beat the living daylights out of us with a huge stick, only for Peter Fitzgerald pulling his Swiss army knife on him and he backed away. He had an orchard, but they were only crab apples and even we wouldn't have bothered stealing them.

Then a miracle happened. That night me and Peter were telling all the lads about our adventure when we heard a tiny little meow. It had just started to rain and this tiny little black and white kitten climbed in through the window. Richard Mooney was the only one asleep and the kitten walked straight across his love letters to Carmel Tucker with her muddy paws and headed straight for Michael Porter and started licking the tears off his face. We were all afraid to move or talk. You could see Michael Porter's eyes blazing in the nearly darkness as she settled by his pillow. You could hear her purring in the stillness. Nobody said a word, but we all knew without saying anything, somehow, somewhere, we were all looked after and we weren't alone. Next day we christened his kitten Muddy Paws.

Everyone grew to love Muddy Paws really fast. She made everyone feel special, with her little pink nose and her black and white face, even Matron, and everywhere Michael Porter went she'd follow a few inches behind. She reminded me of the way Princess (or Tinkerbell) would look at big Jim Clancy when we'd be running in the playground, or playing table tennis, or even just talking, and I knew I could never let her kiss me, even if she wanted to, because I was definitely going to marry Nurse Feeney no matter what happened. She always told me that we couldn't be a real boyfriend and girlfriend while I was still in the hospital so there was another reason I was desperate to get home. Everyone else now had a girl-friend or boyfriend or even a pussycat and was really happy.

They started painting up the whole hospital suddenly one day. We were out playing relievio in the playground; the girls were brutal but I used to let Tinkerbell catch me 'cos she could hardly run. Jim Clancy had never come back to visit her or us. I knew I'd never do that when I got out, especially to Richard Mooney 'cos I'd say he'd be in for life. They'd pulled all the beds with the bedridden patients out into the sun in front of the veranda. They had the best laugh ever, screaming and shouting like at the pantomimes. I even hid in the bed with Richard Mooney and they couldn't find me for ages until he pinched me with his toes and I had to give in. The men painted the whole ward in one day and then we were all given brand new clothes and the barber came in and scalped us. We all knew something huge was up. Two days later Sister Conroy made us all get into bed early. Next thing the Matron who hardly ever came down from the babies' ward except when Derek died, marched in. I was sure it was over everyone feeling Nurse Bannister's bosoms or maybe robbing the orchards, but she started smiling so it wasn't that.

'Boys, I have a very important job for ye to do. There's high men from the government coming to inspect the hospital next Saturday. I want all of ye to either lie or sit quietly on the beds, and answer respectfully anything they ask. Just yes sir and no sir.' On and on she went about how great the nurses were, and how we were lucky to have such lovely food. Michael Porter farted, I don't think he meant it but she pretended not to notice and said what a lovely group of young boys we were. Then all of us who could walk were asked to push all the beds together and they brought in a projector and screen and showed us a film – The Gold Rush. I loved Charlie Chaplin and used to do his walk for Derek any time he needed a bit of a cheering. They even handed around jelly and ice cream and we all had to give three cheers for Matron as she left.

I couldn't sleep that night and knew this was the only chance I'd ever get to go home for good. They must have thought I was taking the whole thing really serious because I had three baths in a row. But what I was really doing was writing a letter to the government. DeValera was his name I think. I remember Uncle Mick saying he was an impostor but I couldn't remember his first name so I just wrote 'Dear Mr President DeValera'. I still had some

Belvedere Bond writing paper and I'd always write with my magical Emerald Street address on the top right-hand corner, but the government people would know it was from a kid in the hospital. I nearly wasted all the writing paper before I finally got it right.

Robbie O'Neill
11 Emerald Street
Seville Place
Dublin
Ireland

19th April 1959

Dear Mr President DeValera,

A terrible mistake has been made. I've been in here now for nearly nine months, and there is nothing wrong with me. My ma is too afraid and Da is too sick to do anything about it. But Da told me you were in jail once, and it was not your fault, so you know what I mean. Please write to the Matron to get me a proper doctor, because my last one died. The nurses here are lovely but you could not eat the food and in any case I have to get home to fix my da.

Yours Faithfully,

Robbie O'Neill
PS Tell Misses President DeValera I was asking for her.

I just wrote 'To the President of Ireland' on the envelope and licked it closed and didn't put on a stamp. I was really nervous, wondering how I'd sneak the letter to the government men, but I knew if I didn't do it, I'd be stuck in here for ever or at least until I was sixteen when they'd send you to Cappagh Hospital and Nurse Feeney might very well get tired of waiting and marry someone else. Michael Porter was the only one I knew who'd been to Cappagh and come out alive, 'cos the boys there were really old and would beat the bejaysus outa you if you didn't get them a bedpan and play with their thing, and I'd certainly rather die than end up there.

That Friday night I put the letter and my picture of Jesus under the pillow. I knew there was no way he'd let me down so I went out to look at the stars. It was easier to see the buses at night-time through the trees, full of loads of people going into town for their Guinness. It wouldn't be long now before I could take Da on a bus into town to the pictures, and Ma would be thrilled when I'd bring him back sober, and there'd be no shouting fights that night. There'd be no more headaches in our house and even Uncle Mick could go back to work with the cattle. After this place, arthritis would be easy to cure if he ever got it back, and maybe Tommy would marry Hattie Hobson, and I'd make sure Shea was top of his class. Ma would never have to go into hospital again with her asthma. Elaine would marry Joe Connolly 'cos he looked so like Elvis, and I might even get a bedroom to myself or with Shea, and I'd teach my baby sister Mary Joe the harmonica and we'd start a harmonica band. Maybe Da could even get a car, it wouldn't have to be a Citroën, and drive me to all the halls where I'd do the faith healing, and they'd all be packed and I'd be famous. Then I could buy my big white house in Howth and marry Nurse Feeney. We'd have enough space for everyone to have a room of their own. A dog was barking, way, way in the distance, and I couldn't wait to get home and bring Bobby to Dollymount and Fairview.

The wind started shivering the trees and I hoped wherever Da was that night that he was wearing his big coat. It couldn't take more than five days for the President to read my letter so I knew I'd be home latest next Friday. I walked through the bushes and said goodbye to the rabbits and wandered back in to tell Richard Mooney my plan. I knew immediately by his face that something was wrong.

'Robbie, the night nurses changed all the sheets for tomorrow. They found a letter under your pillow and brought it straight to Matron and she's been looking for you everywhere. They let this fall.' He handed me my picture of Jesus. 'I heard Matron tell them to get the isolation ward ready.'

My heart thumped so fast I knew there was another massive heart attack on the way. So I lay on the bed for a few seconds and got rid of it. There was no one in the night-nurses' office so I knew they must be out looking for me and I had time to think. Everyone else was asleep except Richard Mooney and I knew by the smell that the new boy on my left didn't know about bedpans and had gone to the toilet in his bed, so I hid under it 'cos I knew the nurses wouldn't come near him and leave the whole mess for the day nurses to sort out. I could easily escape tonight, but my ma would send me straight back so that wouldn't work. I could write the letter all over again and post it because I still had some Belvedere Bond left over, but I'd need a stamp and they'd be watching me like a hawk. The government men would never go to the isolation ward, in case they caught polio. I couldn't think what to do.

I kept staring at the picture of Jesus under the smelly

bed in the dark and it was freezing. I kept thinking of my da in the big coat and the picture smiled back and I got the plan. Richard Mooney said no about five times until he finally agreed. The Matron knew about my letter now and I couldn't wait another second. I wrote the letter out a second time in the bathroom, but this time much more shaky. And I folded up the envelope inside another one addressed to Father Supple – the young priest with the Brylcreem who I hoped wasn't still mad at me for not becoming a priest. I wasn't really afraid 'cos I'd nearly died once before and knew what the whole thing was about.

There was nobody in the night-nurses' office when I stole the sleeping pills. I put the letter inside my sock and broke open the seal off the twenty tablets. I pinched eleven 'cos it was the magic number of my house and hoped it wasn't too much. And anyway Richard Mooney had made me a vow that he'd tell them but not till an hour after I'd taken them. I could hear him crying in the distance after I'd swallowed the tablets and I hoped he wouldn't let me down. I swore if I ever came out of this he'd be my friend for life and could even come to live with me when I bought the big house in Howth.

I knew Latin so well and it wasn't my first extreme unction so when I heard the priest muttering I knew the plan had worked and they must have pumped out my stomach. I couldn't believe how well I felt but found it really hard to talk. I could see the screen and smell the Brylcreem and thank God nobody had taken off my socks. Father Supple couldn't believe it when I whispered my plan in his ear. He reached down and took out the letter and promised he'd get it to the government, and that was the last thing I remembered for all of that night.

There was loads of excitement the next day but I didn't

get to see any of it. The isolation ward was like a hotel. You could get anything to eat that you wanted. But the nurse that sat beside me all day wouldn't even let me out of bed to go to the toilet and I had to use the bedpan and I hated that. The night nurse told me all about the government men. They were real nice to everyone and chatted for ages to all the boys. Matron was delighted 'cos no one had given out about anything, and they had a big party when the men left. I could still hear it going on in the distance, and the night nurse opened the window to let me hear the music but she said she wasn't allowed let me look out.

Ma was the only one let in to see me that Sunday. I don't know what they'd said to her and she never said a thing. Just that Da was on the mend. They sent a man to talk to me every day after that. He wasn't a real doctor because he never mentioned anything about the round shoulders or the flat feet or the head thing. Just chatted for hours, mainly about himself. He seemed very depressed so I told him loads of stories about the hospital to cheer him up and we had a good laugh, but he'd always come back to the Patrick's Day one, the day my head got crushed. Once I very nearly told him about talking to Jesus, and my picture and the way I could make things happen, but stopped at the last minute. I don't know why because he was a very nice man.

Then a fantastic thing happened. I heard him talking outside the door to Sister Conroy and for once there was no nurse in the room. I had my ear up against the keyhole and heard the whole thing. There was nothing wrong with me, nothing at all and I should be sent home straight away. Only then did I realise he was from the government and President DeValera and maybe even his wife must have already read the letter, and my plan had worked. I hopped back into bed and for the next two days was the most obedient kid they ever had in that hospital.

When I was moved back down onto the veranda everything seemed as usual. My bed in the same place and no one had stolen anything from my locker. Richard Mooney said the only change was the food was back to gristle and semolina and the nurses stood beside you when you were taking tablets to watch you swallow them and not keep them to give to someone else. It was sunny every day now, and we were allowed in the playground from morning till night.

Once I'd heard what the man from the government had said about there being nothing wrong with me I knew there could only be a few days left before I'd get out and the place didn't seem such a kip any more. I was lying on the grass near the playground in the hot sun reading a cowboy book called *Lash LaRue*. Tinkerbell and some boys and girls were sitting not far away, pulling petals off buttercups – he loves me, he loves me not. The nurses were sunbathing on the roof of the girls' veranda. Nurse Feeney was putting cream on her legs and they looked all tan and lovely. Sister Conroy was sitting on a deckchair with her white legs stretched out, eating ice cream. The boys' beds were pulled out into the sun but most of them were sleeping. Some other boys were playing cards in the corner of the playground and fighting about who'd won. I could still hear them playing with the buttercups. This time it was the boys' turn – she loves me, she loves me not – and I wondered why Ma had left me in the hospital so long. It didn't matter now and all I could think of was going home and seeing Bobby again and if he was much bigger and if he'd remember me. I'd take him straight to the Phoenix Park. He loved everything about it. The dog pond full of muck that I didn't know about.

I remember the first day I brought him there so well. Ma had loaned me the Brownie camera and I wanted to take all sorts of pictures of him, but it didn't work out as I planned. My conductor friend Mr Murphy who'd let you call him Liam, was on the bus. He'd never seen Bobby before so I got away just that once taking him on the bus. He puked up all over the floor halfway there and there was a terrible smell. It was so bad when Liam came to collect the fares he started getting sick himself. That started off a few other passengers retching away into their hankies and onto the floor. I noticed an older man whose hankie was all brown so he must have been taking snuff like Father McOrly. Bobby was smart enough and crawled a few seats away from the mess, but soon the whole floor of the top deck was covered in vomit and my shoes were all sticky. Mr Murphy was very annoyed and he got the driver to pull in at Cunningham Road garage and made all the passengers get off because he wanted to clean the bus and couldn't stick the smell. But that was OK for me and Bobby because it was right beside the Phoenix Park. But a lot of the other passengers, especially the women with their shopping bags, weren't happy at all and gave out hell to us on the stairs. Mr Murphy told me never to call him Liam again and if he ever saw my bleedin' dog on the road he'd run over him for sure.

Bobby was so excited going to a new park, he nearly choked himself to death. I had to let him off the lead before we even got to the Wellington monument. There was an awful lot of traffic and cars and he ran straight across the road because there was a woman with a walking stick and a white poodle on the other side. Three cars missed him by inches, and I had to put my hands over my eyes. Next minute I could hear the woman roaring because Bobby was doing the horse thing to her white poodle. I ran across and dragged him away. I had to put him back on the lead and drag him to the polo grounds where there wouldn't be any cars and there was loads of space. There was a match on. Guinness's were playing a foreign team, because they all had brown faces. Bobby had calmed down a bit and I'd got him a drink from the iron tap on the side of the road that was very hard to turn on and only a trickle of water came out, but I cupped it in my hand and let him lap away. There were cricket men playing in their white trousers on the other side of the road shouting 'Howzat!' every few minutes. I was dying to go and watch them because I knew I'd be a great batsman when I grew up but I couldn't find Bobby anywhere. That was the trouble any time you took him out, he'd go missing for hours, you couldn't take your eye off him for a minute, but he'd always find his way back when you were standing freezing in the cold and it was getting dark. At least this was a lovely sunny day and all the Guinness men on their horses had posh accents but they still cursed a lot. The thing about polo is you wouldn't want to get hit by their ball 'cos it's so hard and made of wood. I stayed behind the goal and every now and then I'd get a chance to run after it and throw it back. They kept saying, 'Well done, chap,' and I forgot about Bobby for a while.

One of them with a big moustache let me hold his horse's reins when he was changing onto another one, until his wife in a red jacket took over. She looked very young. They even gave me lemonade at half-time and let me go up into the stand to watch. But the next half wasn't started too long when Bobby came charging like mad across the pitch like a champion sheepdog trying to round up the horses. The men on their horses were cursing even worse than any of my cousins. I sneaked down the green wooden stairs of their stand and ran like the wind after Bobby. I grabbed him and didn't stop running until we were back up near the men playing cricket. He kept licking my face as if nothing had happened and afterwards when I told Da he said it was just nature's way, but maybe not to bring him up there again.

The cricket match was much quieter. I had Bobby on the lead now, and he just lay there panting away. Even when I let him off the lead after about half an hour he just lay there quietly, didn't chase the ball and didn't try and bite anybody. They stopped for tea and sandwiches. I was starving so we decided to go home soon, even though I knew there was only stew on. When the cricket men came back out onto the pitch, one of the fielders put his sandwiches down on a piece of tin foil near the little wooden border at the far end, but right beside us. I couldn't take my eyes off them. He was only standing about three yards from us. The men with the bats never hit the ball near him so he never moved. Anyway they were probably egg, and neither me or Bobby would eat those.

It was getting late. The shadows from the trees were stretching across the park. I was a bit afraid that we might meet the same bus men and would have to walk home, so off we went. Bobby was pulling harder than ever, choking and frothing at the mouth. I was too tired to carry him. I knew he was thirsty. We went over to the tap on the side of the road, but this time it wouldn't work at all, no matter how hard I tried. Then I remembered there was a dog pond just through a little forest not far from the gates. I let him off and you'd think he knew. I walked after him because I was too tired to run. There was a few ducks way out in the middle and Bobby was barking at them from the shore. Then I remembered I hadn't even taken one photograph of him. I wanted it to be special so I threw in a big branch of a tree, way out far into the pond, and Bobby went straight in and swam after it. I took some great pictures and hoped it was bright enough. Then he started yelping. He was trying to swim but couldn't move. I thought he was stuck in the mud or the reeds because you could just see the top of them above the water, which was beginning to ripple now with the evening wind. A man with a chocolate brown Labrador on a lead came walking by. 'That dog's in trouble.' But he didn't stop to help. Bobby was barking very loud now and thrashing around. I just couldn't believe it. I'd got him into all this mess. If I ever got him out safely I'd never bring him to this poxy park again and I'd put a blanket in his hut for winter and buy him proper dog food.

It was still bright enough to see the fright in his eyes. I took off my shoes and socks but left my trousers on. I went straight in. I could feel all the mud squelching off my feet and through my toes. The closer I got to him the more it sucked me down. We were very close now but my mouth was barely above the water. The next step I took I went straight under. There must have been a dip or a hole or something 'cos I couldn't get my balance. I knew I was born with a caul and wasn't supposed to drown, but when I came up my eyes were stinging. I couldn't see a thing. Only hear Bobby barking much closer to me now, because he must have broken free when he saw me in trouble. He had the big branch in his mouth. I caught the end of it and he dragged me a few feet back into my depth. Between us we managed to scramble back to the shore. I told Bobby he was the greatest hero ever and I'd get him mince all to himself tomorrow. We were muck all over except for my shoes and socks. We both rolled in the grass as much as we could but there was no chance of getting on a bus. It was a long cold miserable walk home and me and Bobby never went there again.

But it was still lovely and warm here, lying on the grass near the playground. The sun was so bright I couldn't read any more. Nurse Feeney turned over on her back. I hoped she wouldn't get sunburnt. 'He loves you' – all the girls danced around Tinkerbell. But no word from Jim Clancy yet. He was probably busy setting up his new shop. I wondered what the new shop man in Emerald Street was doing. It was so hot all my family'd be out in Dollymount with Da boiling the kettle and looking across the bay at our big white house – if he was well enough, if Ma was telling me the truth. And Uncle Mick, I tried hard to remember his face, and the Reddings – at least they wouldn't get pneumonia today. I could see Mrs Grant now, the old teacher, doddering down amongst the beds in the sun. She loved plays, especially Sean O'Casey's. Then last Easter her putting on that passion play about Jesus. She wanted me to play Judas. But nobody else was fit enough to hang from a cross, so they painted a beard on me. And Nurse Feeney as Mary Magdalene because Nurse Bannister was on holidays. Peter Fitzgerald played Judas and he stole my girlfriend and the show. But on the cross, in the quiet as they played 'Piet Jesu', none of that mattered and that last cry, 'Why hast thou forsaken me?' I wondered if Ma really believed there was something wrong with my head or Da needed special minding from her or was it all a mistake. But maybe she knew I had a special job to do and this was where God wanted me to be.

Sister Conroy had slumped down in the deckchair and I could see her white knickers. The boys were squealing because Richard Mooney kept pinching them with his toes until they paid him the money, and the girls were still playing he loves me, he loves me not and I fell asleep in the sun.

That night I had a great dream. I was a cowboy like Uncle Mick used to be, on a white horse with black cowboy clothes and boots and a white hat. My spurs were silver and I had a Winchester rifle in one hand and a whip in the other and I was helping Uncle Mick drive all the cattle down to the docks and onto his ship. Just as I got back to our house a big black Citroën pulled up and Father McOrly was driving it in his mass clothes, and inside were all my pals from the hospital – Richard Mooney, Jim Clancy, Michael Porter and loads of others – and they were all wearing green jackets and white trousers. Our street was much wider and it was all greasy. Tom Daly still wasn't wearing any shoes but he had a new grey suit and he took over the horse and led him away. Ma and Da were standing at the door of 11 Emerald Street. They were smiling and holding hands and delighted to see me, but our house was so different and huge – just like my big white house in Howth. Nurse Feeney came along with a big tray of ice-cream tubs for everyone. But she winked at me to stay behind and wait until they all had gone laughing inside the house. Ma was last to leave and close the door. Then me and Nurse Feeney sat on the kerb, but it was a hill now with lovely green grass and loads of buttercups. I picked one up and held it under her chin and the evening sun made everything golden. Not just under her chin but the whole street. Tom Daly went by with my big white horse pulling his cart. He looked like a warrior in a chariot. Even the flats in the distance looked like Egyptian palaces as the sun set behind the wall in a rosy glow. Nurse Feeney leaned towards me and her face was as dark and as beautiful as anything you've ever seen. She started whispering to me, 'Robbie, I have to go home now. Robbie, I have to go home.'

Next morning when I woke up early, everything

seemed like my dream — the rosy sun was just rising, slanting rays across everyone's faces and they all looked like peaceful sleeping heroes. There was still dew on the wet grass as I walked across it, making my bare feet wet. When I looked back at the mansion it looked like Camelot with shadows and battlements. Even the birds looked like eagles in the distance, swooping by the huge oak trees. I went into the woods and peed in a huge arc. Then because I hadn't looked in a while, I noticed it was bigger and I'd grown a lot more hair down there. I fed the rabbits and let the big black one out because he loved a chase. I raced through the still wet bushes and remembered my first wet kiss from Nurse Feeney — then I remembered my dream. The night nurses were making their last cup of tea in the office before leaving so I went in to join them. Nurse Feeney was standing there with the others, but they weren't drinking tea. They were drinking champagne. They turned off the music and stopped dancing.

'Say goodbye to your girlfriend, Robbie. She's escaping.' The nurse from Meath, that I'd met that first day, was smirking.

'He looks old enough to have a sip,' the other one giggled.

Nurse Feeney switched the music back on very loud, handed me a glass and whispered, 'Robbie, I tried to tell you last night. I couldn't wake you up. I left you a letter.' Then she swung around and started jiving with the others as if nothing had happened. It was 'Take Me Back to the Black Hills'. I'll never forget it. Any time the others turned away she'd put her hand on my shoulder or squeeze my arm, and the funny thing is I wasn't even sad because I already knew I'd be going home soon and that I would meet her again.

We were allowed stay up the next night to hear Ronny Delaney win the gold medal in Australia, so we made up our own Olympics. Someone brought in a huge ball of twine, and we tied it across the wire fences for the hurdle and the high jumps. They didn't like us doing the long jump because everyone had to get their knees bandaged afterwards. I was second in the marathon behind Peter Fitzgerald and we were both in bare feet, but there was forty-three laps left and I knew I could pass him easy. The sun was blazing and all the kids were in a bunch cheering, even the girls. The tar was soft under my feet. The sweat was going into my eyes. It was a lovely feeling and didn't sting. I knew every corner so well I could close my eyes and look straight at the sun and feel it shining in my face. Even Peter was smiling and it wasn't really a race any more and it didn't matter who won. Outside the veranda, I could see they'd pulled the beds out into the sun again. Everyone in their golden carriage that couldn't move.

Away in the distance a few strangers in bright summer frocks were standing in the shade chatting and smiling with Sister Conroy and watching us all. Then they stood out into the sun and I could see it was my ma with my suitcase and I was finally going home.

We walked down the avenue past the trees in the hot sun. Aunt Chrissie was there just like that first day and she carried my case. The big iron gates were wide open, but rusty, and it wasn't like what I'd always dreamt of. I was glad they were chatting away to each other because I didn't want them to see me sad. I took a last look back at the big mansion, and could still hear my pals cheering. Peter Fitzgerald must have won the race. We waited for ages at the bus stop and I couldn't get used to my new clothes with all the pockets. I had my present from Da, still wrapped in brown paper and string, in the inside pocket. Chrissie said I'd grown up a lot and we went upstairs in the bus and I paid all the fares. The tide was glistening all along Clontarf and there was millions of kids in Fairview Park. Ma didn't mind when I told her I wanted to get off, and she laughed when she warned me not to play football and ruin my new good shoes.

I sat for ages in the flower garden looking out at the cars and buses and thinking about my pals. I hadn't had time to say goodbye properly – just shook everyone's hand. They didn't even stop the race and nobody seemed to notice or mind that I was leaving for ever. Only Richard Mooney with his little feet and a pinch and a smile. Maybe they thought I was on a day excursion. That must have been it. There was kids playing cricket in Fairview with hurleys and I watched for a while. I could lie on the fresh cut grass and close one eye and still count the buttercups and daisies. If I lifted my chin I could see the clock on Gaffney's pub across the road above the traffic. I wanted to wait until a quarter past six 'cos I knew how long it'd take me to run home, and I wanted Da to be home from work and answer the door to my special knock. Then I remembered Da's present. I opened it slowly and carefully. Inside was a beautiful silver telescope and a little card. Da's hand-writing was so clear. 'Robbie – keep searching for the stars.' It was less than a mile to the turn in Clontarf where you could see Howth Head. Through the tele-scope I could see the white house really clear and I couldn't wait to get home to tell Da.

There was nobody on Emerald Street because it was teatime. Once again they'd put new tar on the road. I stood outside number eleven a while wondering what I'd say when Da opened the door. The minute I went to knock, I knew something terrible was wrong. The brass on the letter box hadn't been cleaned for months and the blinds on the parlour window were down. Chrissie answered the door with a big smile and shushed me down the hall, past the parlour door and the Michael Collins picture that Da hated.

Everything in my house in Emerald Street had changed. Uncle Mick was asleep by the fire. Ma and Tommy were sitting at the kitchen table waiting for me to come in. They'd painted all the wallpaper a horrible green. Shea was out walking Bobby and I couldn't believe that.

Then they told me the truth about Da, that he couldn't work any more and wasn't going to get better. I couldn't believe they were so stupid. Even Chrissie wasn't smiling as she held my hand. They'd put a bed in the parlour so Da wouldn't have to climb the stairs and the Christian Brothers in O'Connell's all agreed that we didn't have to pay the fees.

Elaine was out teaching Irish dancing and Mary Joe was in bed with the flu. Tommy got up to turn off Radio Luxembourg on the wireless the minute I came in. He sat back in Da's seat at the table with his hand pencilling out jobs vacant in the paper. Every now and then he'd reach over and touch my shoulder. They were big enough but they weren't like Da's hands.

No one was allowed go into the parlour yet 'cos Da was asleep on the morphine and couldn't be disturbed. I could see all the words coming from everybody's mouths but I couldn't hear anything. I didn't want to so I just closed my ears and went inside my head. Suddenly I was back in that brilliant safe white tunnel and could talk to God. I stayed there until everything was fixed. It was a long time. Then I heard Bobby barking and Shea's knock on the door. Shea whispered the truth to me.

About two hours later Uncle Andy came in to collect Chrissie. He always brought lots of sweets and was delighted to see me. Then Bridie came with all our cousins and we were allowed play late on the street. I saw Uncle Paul, my da's rich brother, pull up in his Anglia car with a huge box of groceries for Ma. Then Uncle Nicky and Willy came along and there was three cars pulled up outside our house, the first time ever! A few neighbours came in and nobody even noticed me slip into the parlour to see my da. It was very dark but a bit of the evening sun came in through the shutters. His little transistor radio was playing 'Red Sails in the Sunset'. I could smell him straight away in the bed in the corner. Not the Guinness or the tobacco or the grease. Just Da's smell. He was fast asleep, I knew by the breathing. I took my picture of Jesus from the back pocket of my new long corduroy trousers. His pillow was wet with sweat but I still managed to lift it a tiny bit and sneak it under. I stood there watching him breathe. I could hear the laughs from the kitchen and the shouts of my pals in the street playing Red Rover. The music on the little transistor had changed to 'Liverpool Lou'. I took my harmonica from my new jacket pocket and played along to the tune, really quietly. I knew it was one of my da's favourites and I could swear I saw him smile. Then I leaned over and barely whispered in his ear how much I loved him and how soon he'd get better, and he definitely whispered back, 'Welcome home, son'. A ball banged off the parlour window and he winced for a split second. I wiped a bit of sweat off his forehead with the cuff of my new white shirt and knew I wasn't home a minute too soon.

Later that night me and Bobby went for a long walk. He didn't pull that hard on the lead now, and was delighted I was home. We stopped on the bridge over the railway and watched the trains shunting and I sat up on the wall. I could see the lights of the cars in the distance coming down the Dublin mountains. I could still smell Da off the cuff of my white shirt. There was even a satellite going by and I wondered would Ma really believe me when I told her I could get God to fix Da.

The next day in the parlour in the morning sunlight Da had got his blazing blue eyes back again and he was smiling. He'd nearly finished all his Complan but his voice was very weak. I had to lean right over to hear what he wanted. When I handed him the wallet he took out a brand new one-pound note, neatly folded. He wanted me to get him a naggin of Jameson and say nothing to Ma. Outside in the street some of Clicky Kelly's gang was hanging around up by the Ball Alley pub and I asked Tommy to come with me. He was huge now and in his last year in school, and he swore he wouldn't say a word to Ma. Inside the pub there was a queue waiting for take-outs. Mainly Guinness in brown bags. I saw Tommy talking to Red Mick in the corner. Red Mick was a martyr for the horses and had the racing page spread on the counter. Tommy came over to me with a mad look in his eyes. He grabbed the pound off me, shouted 'Follow me!' and raced out the door. Down Sheriff Street past the butcher's and the church and Bertie Donnelley's pub. I only caught up with him at the door of Kilmartin's bookies, and begged him not to go in. He said Red Mick had given him five sure things and he was gonna do doubles and trebles and accumulators and win a fortune for Da. He still had that mad look and I knew there was no way of stopping him.

That was the first time I realised Tommy could do magic too. I couldn't listen to the racing results coming through so I sat on the wall of the bridge over the train tracks and all I could think of was Da lying at home gumming for his whiskey. Then Tommy ran out shouting that we had the first one up. I nearly fell off the wall and ran back with him into the bookies. Tommy was walking up and down looking at the race list and listening to the radio voice coming through and every now and then he'd give me a big thump so I knew we were doing well, and that he must have done this before, because loads of the men knew his first name. He was sweating before the four-twenty race and asked me to say a big prayer.

Outside on the street he was in a daze. We sat on the bridge and counted the winnings. Thirty-seven pounds, ten and six, and we couldn't even tell Ma. Then he had a great plan. He was gonna go to O'Connell's school and pay off the school money, mine and Shea's, because he was still on the scholarship and he didn't want us to be beholden to anyone. I was to go back to the Ball Alley, give Red Mick two pounds for his trouble, get Da's whiskey and give Da back the exact change. I could keep a pound for myself and one for Shea. Tommy was going to hang on to the rest for a rainy day and just spend two pounds out of it because he was going out with one of the Royalette girl dancers and she was used to posh restaurants. It was the first time we had a real secret between us and he even said I could have his leather jacket for keeps, it was too small for him. Da must have dozed off because he never asked me what took me so long. He took a sip of the whiskey and lay back with a smile and I hid the naggin under his pillow beside my picture and hoped he wouldn't look.

If things in number eleven had changed a lot, at least the street was exactly the same, except some new people had moved into the house on the corner with the Emerald Street sign high on their wall. They were very nice and didn't mind me banging the tennis ball with the hurley off their wall. The eldest boy, called Jim, was very good-looking and he challenged me to a race around the block on my second day back from hospital. He was a year younger than me but I barely won and decided never to race him again. Their da worked on the railway and could always tell you where the Sunday mystery train was going, so you wouldn't waste your money on a stupid short trip to Newbridge and they wouldn't even serve you in the shops because they thought everyone from Dublin was a robber. One Monday, their da told us that the next Sunday's train was going to Killarney and word must have got out 'cos there were thousands of people queuing up at Kingsbridge station, mostly from our parish, and there was nearly a riot when everyone couldn't get on.

Their younger brother, Frankie, had got a head accident from a belt of a hurley and everybody said he was a bit slow, but he was the only one I'd met that would believe everything I said, and my job was to tell everyone the secret and I told him. He was brilliant at it. I remember the first day I got him to practise and he could do it the first time. It was in Fairview Park, and we were playing football against the East Wall gang from over the bridge. We nearly hated them as much as Clicky Kelly's. We even got a loan of football jerseys off Tommy's team, but it was pissing rain and we were all sheltering under the trees. Frankie was dying to play because one of their cousins from England was over. He was on the English school-boys' team and had to go home the next week, and we all knew if he could play this week we'd hammer them easy. Anyway I got Frankie to help me and we closed our eyes to make the rain go away. It didn't happen straight away and I kept opening one eye to see if there was any sign of the sun peeping out. I was nearly giving up until I saw Frank's face – eyes shut tightly, believing it would happen. Then I knew God wouldn't let him down. Sure enough the rain eased and the match started and it was twelve all near the end, and Frankie got the last goal, the winner, with a header. I was delighted for him and it didn't seem to hurt his head. We carried him home shoulder high, until he got too heavy for us, and we were all so excited we never noticed that the East Wallers had stolen our ball.

The next day Da was fast asleep in the parlour. I'd wiped away the sweat on his forehead again and he never woke up. There was a pedal on the piano to soften the sound and I pushed it straight down hard. I was playing away quietly with one finger making sure I wouldn't wake him. It didn't take me long to pick out all the old tunes I used to be able to play. I had a go at 'Slieve na mBán'. At least it was a Tipperary song. It was Sunday afternoon and everyone had left the house. Only Uncle Mick was still in the kitchen, writing down the scores of the match on the back of the cornflakes box. Tipperary were playing Kilkenny in a big final. I wanted so much for Tipp to win but I couldn't listen to all the match. I just sneaked in to the kitchen to ask Uncle Mick what was the score about every ten minutes. It was very close. Just a point or two between the teams, so I'd go back into the parlour and play every single Tipperary song I could think of.

Then something dawned on me that I'd thought of when I was in the hospital one night, lying in bed and crying because I thought that Nurse Feeney didn't love me any more. I was thinking of the wedding photograph of Ma and Da on the piano. My eyes were closed tight and I could see them in their lovely clothes and holding hands nervously. I remembered there was something wrong with the photograph. But now, here it was in front of me again. I took it down and tried to study it in the half light as the evening closed in. Ma in her black suit with the lovely hat and the feather, Da in the suit that he'd told me was really brown. Ma was wearing a rose that looked white but could have been maybe yellow. And then I saw it. She wasn't wearing the same wedding ring.

The one she had now was big and fancy with a massive stone in the middle that Da's mother left her when she died. Da was very keen Ma would wear it because her first one was so skinny. I heard Ma telling Theresa that she didn't really want it and only wore it to please Da. The one in the photograph was just a thin band of gold, like something you'd find in a Halloween barmbrack.

Mr Ross was the man who took Ma and Da's wedding photograph. He thought it was so good he kept it in his shop window for years. When they were married first and had no money to go to the pictures, they'd get my da's mother to mind Elaine and walk up into Henry Street where Mr Ross's shop was and look in at the picture. When Da would drink a lot of Guinness he'd always tell me how lovely Ma looked at their wedding and I'd heard Nurse Feeney say how handsome my da was that night I pretended to be asleep, so Mr Ross must have been a great businessman and I'd say he got a lot of work from that picture of Ma and Da.

Our whole family always got all our communion and confirmation pictures taken by Mr Ross, and even though their wedding photograph was gone from his shop window now, he'd never charge Ma the full price because he was such a nice man. He had a little church kneeler in his shop when he'd be taking your communion or even your confirmation picture, although he only took my communion because he was dead before I was eleven, but at least he got Elaine and Tommy's confirmation one. You had to kneel and be very still and look really holy with your ivory communion beads that Aunt Chrissie had bought us hanging between your hands. He gave every boy and girl sixpence for the communion and a shilling for your confirmation. I was very sad that he died before mine. They kept Elaine's confirmation photograph in the window for years as well, and when me and Da would go up to Henry Street to see the Christmas lights, you could look in at it and it was still there. Mr Ross's son who took over when he died promised me that when Mary Joe's time came, he'd look after her very well, and then he'd laugh and say he hoped he'd be still around to do our weddings. I was sure Tommy was his best bet for that! But I always thought Da should have gone back for another photograph when Ma got the granny's ring. Maybe they were too old then, and too long married to hold hands.

My communion photograph was really funny. I looked much fatter then but still had the same smile. Under my right eye there was a scar because I was still accident prone then. That's what my Uncle Andy said, before he was my uncle and married Chrissie. I remember slipping in the toilet in our backyard that had no lights and bashing my eye off the toilet bowl. He carried me all the way to the chemist's to get plasters. He always wore lovely white shirts because he had a big job in Aer Lingus, and it got covered in my blood. It was only a week to my First Holy Communion. They'd got me a brand new prayer book with a leather cover, that you could see in my communion photograph, along with the cut under my eye. Mr Ross had borrowed some make-up off Ma and did his best, but you could still see the scar. I was very sad to hear when he died before my confirmation, and me and Da always said a prayer for him when we were on our walks, watching the trains shunting, as well as all the people that Da knew who were dead and gone, and even for his brother Mossy who never came back to see us, after that time in our house. Maybe I'd made a bad wish that night, or maybe he just liked being on his own.

Da was definitely getting better now and I was able to take the picture back. We all gave him a big cheer the first day he was able to walk up to the pub on his own. The doctors had been very surprised the way he was putting on weight and told him the odd pint wouldn't do him any harm at all, at least that's what he told Ma and she seemed happy enough about it. The way they were getting on now and the way she looked after him, it was the first time I realised they must still be in love. Every Friday he'd meet his pals from his job in Store Street and they'd buy him a few pints but he never came home drunk. Every time Tommy got a chance he'd slip a few bob into Ma's purse out of the winnings. She never seemed to notice, or maybe she thought it was a miracle because she never missed seven o'clock mass every morning.

There was only a few weeks left in school after getting out of hospital before the summer holidays so I didn't go back. I'd nearly missed a whole year so they told Ma they'd keep me back in the same class to let me catch up. I hated the thought of it but decided not to argue about it 'cos Ma had enough on her plate and anyway it was nearly summer and I'd be getting my first real job.

It was way out in the country in a hospital in Clonskeagh. I had to get the bus out there the first day until they gave me the messenger-boy's bike. It was ten shillings a week and Ma said I could keep five bob for myself. You had to pick up the blood samples from loads of hospitals all over Dublin and bring them back to be tested. But the best part was first thing in the morning I had the gate lodge to myself and I had to make tea for the porters and give them biscuits, and I could eat as many as I wanted. The first week I got lost loads of times, especially in James Street hospital. That was as big as Croke Park and had seven different laboratories and it could take hours to find the right one, but I loved going there 'cos you could freewheel at sixty miles an hour down Christchurch Hill and hop onto the path and miss all the lights.

But the great part of it was I knew that all those little sealed bottles in my messenger-boy's bike, wrapped up in padded parcels, could be life or death for people and I'd break the world record on my Tour de Dublin and every time I handed each one over I'd feel the heat from my hands go straight into them and hope that the people and their families would be getting good news. They always had the name of the patient and the hospital and I'd wonder were they young or old and what were they in for, but I never got in to see any of them so I never knew.

You only had to work a half day on Saturday. I cycled straight home and swapped my messenger-boy's bike for the brand new red one that Da had bought me and that I hadn't used in nearly a whole year. Nobody in our house had taken it out, not even once. They'd put two big sacks over it in the back kitchen so it wouldn't get scratched or rusty. Then I'd cycle straight up to the Phoenix Park, but never with Bobby, and only stop once to buy a bottle of orange and a cream cake. You could watch cricket and polo and sometimes a bike race.

One Saturday I couldn't resist. The cyclists were always in a bunch for the first few laps. I'd borrowed Tommy's green football jersey and white shorts and was pretending I was just cycling down the road minding my own business. They flew past, about a hundred of them and maybe a few stragglers. I never tried so hard in my life and caught up with the back of the bunch. Once you were up to full speed it wasn't that hard, especially when you got the hang of the new gears. For nearly two laps I pretended I was Shay Elliot and even passed two of the racers. Then I went straight out the main gates and cycled home. I had to go to bed real early that night, my legs were so sore.

Sometimes you had to deliver X-rays and you weren't allowed use the bike. They'd give you money for a taxi and you had to get a receipt so you'd know it was a fatal emergency, and you'd have to pray hard for them and hope the taxi man wouldn't talk too much.

Tommy's job was going well too. He was working in Merchant's warehousing for the summer and he was very good at science so he was moved up into the grain moisture office where you had to weigh samples, and he was being paid loads of money and going to the Paradiso Restaurant every Saturday night late with his posh girlfriend that he'd never let you meet. Shea was selling programmes in Croke Park every Sunday and making a right few bob, and wouldn't take any money back off Ma. Elaine had her own Irish-dancing class now and loads of boys used to go as well. She'd never tell you how much she was making, but once I saw her handing loads of pound notes to Ma and her and Joe Connolly were getting on great. He really was the image of Elvis and they started up a band called 'Joe and Elaine' and played Harry Belafonte songs all over Dublin, and even got paid. Mary Joe practised all the time at the harmonica so one day we could be famous too.

I was enjoying my messenger-boy's job so much, I hadn't thought about girls for a long time after coming out of the hospital in Clontarf. They all seemed so giggly and silly that I couldn't be bothered. And I hadn't forgotten Nurse Feeney. Anyway I loved earning the few bob and arriving out in Fairview Park late in the evenings to play football with my pals, even though I kept my promise to my ma and wouldn't heady the ball. Maybe it was all the running and cycling but I was getting really good at the football. Even when my pals weren't there, I'd go up to a bunch of strangers playing a practice match and ask them was there any chance of a game. Most of them would be wearing proper shirts and jerseys but they wouldn't mind you playing in your clothes.

Stella Maris was the best team in Dublin and one day they were practising there. They were short a few because their boys were on holidays so they let me play. I knew I was doing brilliant because I could hear some of the men who ran the club, and brought them out to the match in their car, talking about me. I knocked down three of their players near the sideline but kicked the ball a few inches wide. Then I heard one of them, who I knew was the manager because he had a notebook, saying 'Who the fuck is yer man?' The other boys were all under fourteen but I was still just about under twelve. They even had their own goalie nets for practice matches and three brand new footballs and I'd love to have joined them.

All the older boys were very nice to me after the game and said I was a little dinger, but one of them with long sideburns was a bit annoyed with me and said it was only a fucking friendly practice match and if I wasn't careful someone would break my fucking leg. The manager came over and asked me who was I signed for. He told me to call him Kit and afterwards some of the lads told me he was a very famous footballer in his youth and had played for Shamrock Rovers. He said I was a natural and they were short a player or two for a big cup match the next Saturday down the country in Navan. I signed this long green form he had and knew I could never tell Ma, except if I didn't heady the ball I wouldn't be letting her down.

We were supposed to meet the next Saturday outside the Sunset Bar in Summerhill. I had to tell Ma a big lie about having to work all day and I sneaked Tommy's football boots out without him seeing me. The only thing I had that was big for my age was my feet so they fitted me properly. We were all hanging around outside the pub waiting for the special bus to collect us to the match. All the lads seemed to have girlfriends or mots, as they call them, and what they weren't doing to them was nobody's business. I was dying to tell them about Nurse Feeney, but I couldn't let her down even though I hadn't heard from her in months, so I pretended it was me who'd pulled down Lily Downey's knickers and they got a great laugh out of that. There was a proper dressing room on the pitch and Kit the manager handed me the number eleven jersey so I felt much happier. But the big boy with the long sideburns who'd threatened me before started laughing at my skinny white legs when I put the shorts on. Kit came over and gave me some Wintergreen to rub on them and told him to shut up. When we came out on the pitch the other team looked huge. I was sick in my stomach and wished I'd gone to the toilet and there was loads of spectators in raincoats and holding umbrellas. They even had a rope all around the sidelines and a proper referee in black, and two sideline men. I just remembered to say a special prayer to God that I wouldn't make a show of myself before the referee blew the whistle. It was their tip-off.

I don't know how, but as true as God I knew they'd hit the ball straight back to their centre half to belt it upfield, and that's exactly what happened except I ran straight for him before the ball reached him. I tapped it round him and had the ball in the back of the net in less than five seconds. They must have thought they were after signing Stanley Matthews. But they were so wrong. That was the best thing I ever did on a football pitch ever. I got away with not having to heady the ball once, and I kept out of trouble. We won one nil and I was a bit of a hero, but I think Kit the manager saw through me because he asked me afterwards had I ever played a real football match before.

We were all heading for the dressing room, mucky and tired. The rain had stopped and the sun was starting to shine through. They were all shouting well done Robbie and slapping my back. I kept my eyes staring at the ground, because that's what Stanley Matthews always did when he'd had a great game. Then I heard a girl's voice shouting my name. It was Nurse Feeney. I hardly recognised her in her short summer frock without the nurse's uniform. I'd forgotten she'd gone down to work in the hospital in Navan. Her eyes melted my heart. I couldn't speak. She gave me a big hug and a twirl. The lads were jeering like mad, and my enemy on our team came right up beside us and said, 'Will she be giving you a French kiss?' I knew by her face she was annoyed, so we just walked back up the field.

She was delighted to see me. We had a great chat. I told her all about the new job and she thought it was great. Then she asked me how everyone was in Clontarf hospital and remembered all their names. She was more beautiful than ever, and I was glad I hadn't fallen in love with anyone else. Then she leaned slowly towards me, her lips so soft I wanted the kiss to last forever. Then a big boy came over, even older than my brother Tommy, and called out in a country voice, 'C'mon Roisin, time to go home.' I hoped it was her brother and it was the first time ever I'd heard her real name. But our bus was leaving and I never asked her for her address, especially with her brother around. I sat in the back all the way home. I was as happy as I'd ever been, and had completely forgotten about Da.

Lying in bed that night I started thinking about the

whole thing. I was good at maths and knew that when we got married, say I was twenty, she'd be about twenty-six or seven. But Mrs Hobson – the Protestant woman on our road – was a good fifteen years older than her husband – so Ma said – and everyone said Mr Hobson was a bit of a gold digger because his wife owned all the houses in Emerald Street and collected all the rent. But she was very kind and if there was anything wrong with the houses, like a slate blown off, she'd get it fixed straight away and pay for the whole lot herself. Maybe I could even get her to give me back all my savings for the bike that I had to spend fixing the Reddings' fanlight. Then I could keep the money for my wedding suit and we could use the Christmas present that I never gave her as the wedding ring. And anyway Mr and Mrs Hobson seemed the best of pals. They were always laughing and holding hands and going for their few drinks up in the North Star Hotel in Amiens Street. But their daughter Hattie who was my first girlfriend until Tommy stole her was beautiful and maybe me and Nurse Feeney's children would be just the same, but I'd want to bring them up as Catholics, even though I wasn't sure about the whole thing. We'd get them all baptised anyway, just in case, and let them make up their own minds when the time came. Sure even when I was seventy, she wouldn't even be as old as Uncle Mick, and he could still hop around like a two year old except when he was pretending to have arthritis.

But I was right about one thing. The next Tuesday when I went out to Fairview Park to practise with my new team, Stella Maris, Mr Kit called me aside and said it might be better if I played with the twelve-year-olds, I might find it easier. He must have been joking – they were about the same size as me but they were like animals. I don't know who they were trying to impress but I got kicked left right and centre. I gave as good as I got, but a little skinny blond fella called Damo gave me the greatest kick in the balls with his studs and it was ten times worse than the pain on Da's bike on the way to Drogheda. I blacked out for a few seconds and when I woke up I was vomiting and Mr Kit was looking inside my shorts to make sure I still had two left. The pain didn't go away for nearly two days. I knew things down there had to be in working order to have Nurse Feeney's babies so I decided to give the whole thing up and that was the end of my soccer career.

Da was due his first big visit back to hospital and everyone was nervous. He looked great in his suit. It nearly fitted him again. Ma and Chrissie and Bridie had done the ten-day novena in Gardiner Street and Ma was still very nervous. But Da wasn't. He winked at me on my way out to work on my bike and said I looked nearly big enough to have a pint, and not to worry he'd be in for only two days. Ma had packed way too much of his things and I hoped he wouldn't notice that she was afraid to believe. Mary Joe stood at the door that morning and asked me to come home early and prac- tise our new song.

It was raining nearly all that day in my hospital and there was only one trip for me to Cherry Orchard, so me and the porters played cards nearly all day. I cycled home through the rain and the traffic and Ma had a big fry for all of us, but she looked a bit sad. She swore there was no news and Tommy cancelled his date that night. Shamrock Rovers were playing a big match against a Spanish team on the radio, but nobody was really listening and we went to bed early. I was reading my book but Shea asked me to put out the light so I told him a ghost story instead.

The next day a miracle happened. I was in early and

Mr McGurk, who was the boss of the whole hospital, called me into his office. It was an X-ray day and I'd be spending the whole day in taxis. He gave me five pounds and made sure I'd keep all the receipts, but his brother Paddy who ran the clay-pigeon shooting was looking for a smart young lad to help out next weekend up in Ashbourne, and I could get a lift there both days, and I needn't come in on Saturday and I'd get at least ten bob! I was so happy. I chatted away to the taxi men all morning and forgot to pray for the X-ray people. I was on my last run up to the Mater Hospital when I noticed the name and address: James O'Neill, 11 Emerald Street, c/o Mater Hospital. We were stuck in traffic and we were just in the middle of talking about the Shamrock Rovers match when I noticed the name and address.

'Excuse me, mister, if you can get to the Mater Hospital in five minutes I'll give you an extra shilling.' He was better than Fangio – footpath, side streets, even broke red lights. I made a mistake – I gave him four shillings, all my change, but I didn't care. I knew exactly where to go and told the radiologist it was for a vital urgent fatal case. She took one look at me and ran down the corridor. There was nothing I could do but wait. I went up to St John's ward where Da had been when I escaped from the other hospital, but he wasn't there. There was a man in casualty on a stretcher but it wasn't him. I wandered the whole hospital but wouldn't let God down by peeping into the morgue. Maybe he was home already, or maybe sent off to the hospice. There was a man smoking in the waiting room and I asked him for a loan of a cigarette to have ready for Da. I was pacing outside in the car park when I saw them through a frosted window. Ma and Da laughing and a doctor holding up the X-ray. I was in the door in seconds. They all looked around and the doctor stood up, and Ma explained who I was.

'Well, young sir,' – great, the doctor was still smiling – 'if your father had been to Lourdes, this would have to be declared a miracle. Look, the tumour is gone!' I could only look at Ma's face and Da's face. I hated crying in front of them but what else could I do. On the way home we stopped off in the taxi at Doyle's corner for a pint. Da couldn't stop grinning. He winked at me to have a sip and even though I know Ma saw me, she couldn't even care. When things calmed down I saw the love in his eyes. Just like me, he'd got a second chance.

One day before my messenger job was over I got a great idea. Mondays were always quiet because the test doctors would have had the weekend off, so you could sit around and chat and play cards with the porters and the van drivers nearly all day. One of them, Mr O'Keefe, was my favourite, and even though he told dirty jokes I liked him the best and always kept him one of my cheese sandwiches. I'd been telling him all about the hospital in Clontarf and he loved the stories about Nurse Bannister letting you feel her diddies, even though he called them tits in his jokes. I told him I was dying to go and see my pals out there in the big hospital but you were only allowed visit on Sundays between two and four, and I couldn't go then 'cos I had to go to the pictures. So one Monday he made a fake document up for me to go and collect a urine sample out there and he said he'd cover for me but I had to get Nurse Bannister's address for him and if I did I could spend the whole day. No matter how fast you run it's much quicker on a bike and anyway it was great practice for me when I'd be in the Tour de France.

I couldn't believe how delighted everyone was to see me. It wasn't at all like the day that I left. Sister Conroy was a bit confused about the docket, but she said she'd go and check, and I wasn't to be in any hurry off, and to make sure I stayed for a cup of tea with her, and a chat and maybe even have dinner with them, but I told her I'd already eaten loads of sambos 'cos I certainly didn't want that. Down outside the veranda they were playing Red Rover but when they saw me they all stopped and ran over. We sat on the grass and I told them all my news, but I was dying to go into the ward to see Richard Mooney. There was a new boy in my place and he was getting a bed bath from two nurses I'd never seen before. And there was Richard Mooney sitting in his bed in the corner reading a book and turning the pages with his feet. He roared crying the minute he saw me and couldn't stop 'cos he thought he'd never see me again.

We talked for ages and he told me stuff I'd never heard before. His ma had died at childbirth and he'd never seen his da – not even once, and didn't know if he was alive or dead. He'd been brought straight to the babies' ward in the hospital and then the saddest thing I ever heard. He'd never been outside the hospital – not even once – not even at Christmas when I'd thought he'd gone home. They'd taken him back up into the babies' ward because a lot of the nurses were sent home and it was easier to keep an eye on him up there. All his visitors were from the Quakers and he'd always pretend they were his family because he didn't want to let himself down. It was hard to hug him without his arms, but I did, and I swore, in a whisper, I'd get him out at least for one day. I didn't know how yet but I knew I wouldn't break that vow. He cheered up a bit then but I don't think he really believed me.

Then Michael Porter came up on his crutches and I gave him a big hug too and the three of us started playing cards. I showed them some of the card tricks that my friend Mr O'Keefe the porter had shown me and then I remembered about Nurse Bannister's address, just as she came up behind me and put her hands over my eyes and said 'Guess who!' I wasn't stupid because I could feel her pulling my head back into her big bosoms. She said I was to come with her because Sister Conroy wanted to see me in her office.

I winked at my pals and told them I'd see them next Sunday at visiting time and went off with Nurse Bannister. She stopped and gave me a big kiss in the corridor outside the door of the gym and let me squeeze each of them twice for old times' sake. Peter Fitzgerald came out the door and caught us but didn't say anything for a while. I didn't give him a hug, just shook his hand and told him I'd have a proper chat with him next Sunday. The way he stared at us walking down the corridor I knew even he missed me a bit.

Sister Conroy gave me my third hug of the day and I noticed for the first time that she had big ones too. When I told her about my job, she said I was a credit to the hospital and to come back any time day or night, and that's when I got the idea of how to keep my vow to Richard Mooney. I think she knew the docket thing wasn't real because she never mentioned it once during our tea and Mikado biscuits, and made me promise to come back soon and say hello to Matron.

All that week I stayed up really late making the boxcar in our back kitchen. All Uncle Mick's tools were there – hammer, rusty saw, nails and three tins of paint. Da had loads of trolley wheels and ball bearings from cars and trucks that he always thought would come in useful, and they certainly did. I wasn't bad as a carpenter 'cos I'd made the crib from plywood the year before. Nobody asked me any questions about all the hammering every night, not even Ma. I think she was glad I wasn't out like Shea and Tommy chasing girls and never said a word.

Uncle Mick would wander down every so often, and he was so impressed he said he might give up all the repair work around the house. He gave me the price for a tin of red paint without saying a word to anyone.

When I told my friend Frank O'Keefe the plan he said he'd borrow the van next Sunday for an hour and drive me and the boxcar out to Clontarf but make sure this time I didn't forget to get Nurse Bannister's address.

Rob Roy was on in the Strand Picture House, but I'd made a vow so I didn't feel even a bit sorry when we drove out that Sunday past the big queue. We arrived about three o'clock. All the visitors were already inside as I pulled the boxcar up the avenue and hid it behind a bush outside the veranda garden gates. Now the big problem – could I trust Peter Fitzgerald? I needed him to carry Richard Mooney out to the boxcar. They'd get very suspicious if they saw me do it, and anyway I'd have to divert attention.

I needn't have worried. Once I explained everything, it went like a military plan, and I had to stop Richard Mooney screaming with delight until we were in the van and past the Clontarf Cricket Ground on our way to the coast. He'd never seen the sea before, only on postcards from the Quaker people when they'd been on holidays in Brighton and somewhere else, and he didn't care the way people were looking at us. He begged me to bring him into the sea near Clontarf baths, but I had no towel. I bought him an ice-cream cone and crisps and we had a picnic for about half an hour. Peter Fitzgerald was waiting anxiously at the gate when we got back and no matter what he ever did to me, I knew when I saw him carrying Richard Mooney back in that he would always be a good pal.

If you saw Richard Mooney's face when he saw the sea you'd know you could never let him down, so I didn't get to the Strand cinema again for months. *Lady and the Tramp*, Audie Murphy, Satchmo – I missed them all. Frank O'Keefe was getting fed up with me for not getting Nurse Bannister's address and he stopped driving me out in the van. Bobby my dog couldn't understand why I wasn't bringing him to Dollymount and my arms were nearly pulled out of my sockets pulling Richard Mooney around in the wooden chariot, but I didn't care. He loved Fairview Park the best, and my pals from Emerald Street, the minute they heard what I was up to, used to give me a hand. We'd even have a special match for him and give him a jersey and let him play in goal. But one Sunday evening when Peter Fitzgerald met us to carry him back to his bed, he told me to wait outside, that there was a problem. He was finally being let go home and there would be nobody left strong enough to sneak Richard Mooney in and out. Michael Porter had had a go but fell over his crutches and nearly broke his plaster cast.

I knew I had to come up with a new plan, but at least Peter Fitzgerald had got Nurse Bannister's address so maybe Frank O'Keefe might give us a hand. But for some reason once he got the address he seemed to be very busy every Sunday afternoon so that didn't work.

I was lying in my bed that night with my picture of Jesus under the pillow when I got the answer. What if Richard Mooney came to live with us! So simple – so perfect. He was only in hospital because there was nobody else to mind him. Da was better now and there was nobody sleeping in the parlour. I would play the piano for him every night before he fell asleep and tell him ghost stories. Elaine was going steady now with Joe Connolly and everyone said they'd be married soon, and Tommy was in his last year at school and told me he wanted to get a job down the country straight away so there'd be lots of room. Or maybe he could even stay in the bedroom with me and Shea and we'd have a great laugh. And it would only be for a while because once we found his father he'd be taken off to a big house down the country maybe, not Meath or Laoise though, maybe Carlow, and I would visit him every summer, me and Michael Porter, maybe even Peter Fitzgerald, and he'd never be lonely.

But it wasn't that simple. Elaine told me to mind my own business about when she was getting married. I don't think she ever really forgave me over the golliwog thing. And Tommy said he'd love to help but it depended on his exam results, and anyway it was very dangerous to get involved with cripples. It was the first time I ever gave him a punch and he was very surprised about that, but he didn't hit me back and said he was sorry and he'd do what he could. Shea was brilliant. He came up with a great idea – 'Give it a go over Christmas, Ma would never say no to that, sure she was nearly an orphan herself.' After that I always knew Shea was the real brains of the family, and he was right. But I had to pick the right moment.

One Friday I got home early. Ma asked me to go up and get chips for everyone. Da had got word from the doctors that he could go back to work next Monday, and Ma asked me to get a chocolate Swiss roll from Darcy's on my way back. They were laughing at the kitchen table and Da was listening to the stock exchange report on the wireless. He always did that. When I asked him did he own any shares, Ma burst out laughing and said, 'Yes son, half of Guinness Brewery!' There was no one else around, so I knew this was my chance, and I blurted out my plan.

'What's one more mouth to feed?' they both said together. Just that simple and all my worrying was over. Shea didn't know what was going on when I gave him my slice of chocolate cake.

The next Sunday I was first in the visitors' queue when they opened the gates at two o'clock. When I told Richard Mooney he nearly had an attack of the palsy. He started jumping up and down on the bed like a yo-yo and couldn't talk at all. His eyes were rolling and he started sweating. When I calmed him down he started to talk and shout non-stop.

'Now, now, do it now! I'm sick of the tapioca and I love the smell of the sea. The summer'll be gone soon. Now – I can't wait, please, Robbie. I might be dead, Christmas is ages and I want – I want to go to the bumpers in Bray and they close in winter – go on, ask Matron now, please, please don't say no – oh God I've started wetting myself.' And all the time he was talking he was pinching and thumping my arms with his foot. Then he started coughing and nearly got sick so he had to stop talking. I thought Ma and Da wouldn't mind, but it was all very sudden. I told him it would be better if I got Ma in to talk to Matron but he burst out crying and begged me to go straight to her office now. I did and it was the biggest mistake of my life. At first she hardly recognised me and I had to remind her who I was. She was having a row with someone on the phone and told me to sit down and wait. When she slammed down the phone I told her about Richard Mooney and the plan and how my ma and da would love to have him for a week or two. She nearly went berserk and started shouting at me.

'Are you out of your mind! He needs constant care by professionals!' and other things that I still can't remember except the threat. Was I suffering from the head thing again, and if I wasn't careful I'd be back in the hospital myself!

I stood outside the veranda and knew I could never tell Richard Mooney the truth. When my face wasn't red

any more I went back up to his bed and muttered something about her not being in the office and anyway it'd
be better to get my ma in to ask her. He wasn't stupid.
He knew something was wrong. He went very quiet but
he didn't cry. He just asked me to get my ma in real soon
and that he wanted to go to sleep now.

On the way out I got Michael Porter to come to the
gate with me and told him everything. He promised he'd
keep an eye on Richard Mooney and not let him near
any pills. Ma said she wasn't surprised when I told her
about the Matron, and even though I begged her, she
insisted that it was better to let things settle and she'd
write to the Matron closer to Christmas and maybe get
Father McOrly from our parish to go over with her when
the time was right. But I'd seen that look in Richard
Mooney's eye and I was afraid he would do something
desperate. I realised I couldn't wait until the next Sunday
even though all I had was bad news. I'd have to tell him
sometime when there was no visitors around.

I decided to break in on Saturday night when most of
the nurses would be at dances or out with their boyfriends.
I said a special prayer that Matron would be out with
hers 'cos if she caught me she'd definitely lock me back
up.

At least it wasn't raining and I didn't cut myself climbing
over the fence this time. I could see the lights of the
nurses' office shining out along the boys' veranda as I crept
closer. There was no one around and all the boys seemed
to be asleep, even the new boy in my bed. Michael Porter
was propped up with all the special pillows that they
always gave him. But there was no one in Richard
Mooney's bed! Empty! No toys on his locker – nothing
– as if he was never there. My heart was thumping faster
now but not from fear of being caught. I slid the side
corner window open and slipped inside. His locker door

squeaked as it opened. Nothing inside. 'Pssst!' An urgent whisper from up the ward.

'Pssst! Robbie!' I'd forgotten that Michael Porter was such a night owl. I crawled up to him, shaking, terrified to hear the news.

'He's gone, Robbie, and he's never coming back.' It was the first time Michael Porter had seen me cry. I didn't hear another word he said even though he kept talking. All I could see was Richard Mooney's smiley face that day in Clontarf when the sun was shining as he dipped his bare feet into the cold sea, and they went numb on him and I didn't even have a towel, and what it must have been like for him at Christmas up in the babies' ward pretending he'd been taken home. Michael Porter was still droning on, something about a big house in Terenure called Brookfield, with an orchard and loads of rooms and a library with every book in the world, and they'd get a special wheelchair built for him with electric buttons that Richard Mooney could control with his feet, and suddenly, the blood came back into my head and my fingers and I asked Michael Porter to tell me the whole thing again.

Richard Mooney had stayed in bed without talking to anyone until the previous weekend when Matron and Sister Conroy came down all smiling with new clothes for him. They washed him, and got him dressed, and combed his hair. Then they told him he had visitors and carried him out of the ward. It was raining and all the boys were inside playing cards and blind man's buff, but they stopped when they saw what was going on. Michael Porter thought they were taking him off for experiments, but when they heard the roars and laughs of him as Nurse Bannister carried him back into the ward, they knew something great had happened for him. The Chief of the Quakers and his wife were adopting him and taking him straight away to their big mansion in the country in Terenure in Dublin. Michael Porter said it all happened so quick they hardly had time to say goodbye, and Richard Mooney had shared out all his toys amongst all the boys, and the Chief of the Quakers had come down. He was a lovely man, and told them he was sending in a television set for both the boys' and girls' ward and they could watch pictures all day, but only if they were bedridden, because exercise was important, and Richard Mooney barely had time to whisper to Michael Porter to tell Robbie he'd write him a letter to the hospital in seven days' time, and that me and Michael Porter were allowed visit him any time we wanted and that the Chief of the Quakers had made Matron agree that Michael Porter could spend Christmas in their house. And Michael Porter said that was something, but he missed Richard Mooney already and now all his pals had left and he felt terribly lonely, so I swore a vow to him that the minute I got Richard Mooney's letter with the address, that me and him would go straight out there to the mansion in the country and Matron couldn't say no. It's hard to hug somebody in a plaster cast all over their body except their legs. But I nearly broke it that night and stayed with Michael Porter for ages planning our trips and he was laughing so much he begged me to go.

On my way home, once I climbed back over the wire, I was the happiest I'd been for ages and was thinking if I ever gave up being a Catholic again, I'd definitely become a Quaker. I was passing the nurses' home just beside the hospital when I saw something really strange. It was the van Frank O'Keefe used to borrow from my hospital job and I wondered what was it doing there. The van seemed to be moving a bit from side to side. Then I heard Nurse Bannister's voice shout Frank O'Keefe's name out real loud. I guessed they were having a party, drinking loads of Guinness and maybe she was letting him feel her diddies from the inside. I was so happy I couldn't resist it.

The windscreen was all fogged up so I knew they'd never see me. I still had Peter Fitzgerald's pen and paper in my pocket. I always carried them with me now because I was training to be a writer as well as a faith healer. I just wrote 'Robbie was here' and stuck it under the windscreen wiper, then ran down Castle Avenue, laughing to myself. I hoped Frank O'Keefe wouldn't get too drunk and be able to drive home safely, and not make a show of himself in front of his ma, if she was still alive.

It was a lovely night and when I turned onto Clontarf Road I could see the whole city lit up by the full moon in the clear sky. Through my telescope I counted seventeen spires beginning at our church, St Lawrence O'Toole's near the docks, all the way up to the one beside Dalymount Park. You could see the dark shadow of the Dublin mountains and a few car lights weaving slowly up and down, sometimes pointing up into the dark blue sky. The footpaths through Fairview Park were dappled with tree shadows and shone like sheets of tar.

I had a tingle in my tummy so strong I had to lie on the grass. I closed my eyes. It was a lovely feeling. The happiest I'd ever been. Da was better. Ma was laughing again. Uncle Mick telling his stories. Richard Mooney was lying happy in his new bed in a mansion halfway up the mountains, Michael Porter was dreaming of all the magical Christmases to come, and Frank O'Keefe would be my friend forever. I stood up on the hill and looked back again across the city for the last time that night. Tommy and Elaine were out somewhere with a girlfriend and a boyfriend that they loved. Mary Joe and Bruno her teddy bear were having happy dreams of songs to write and music to play. Shea was kissing all his girlfriends goodnight, and Nurse Feeney was waiting for me. A night wind began to rustle the trees so gently all across the city, so I made a last wish to the magical evening stars.